DELIVERYWOMAN

# DELIVERYWOMAN

*Hope you enjoy!*

## EVA WYLES

*xx*

Influx Press
London

Published by Influx Press
www.influxpress.com
@InfluxPress

Published by Influx Press, London, UK, 2025
© Eva Wyles, 2025

The right of Eva Wyles to be identified as the author of this work has been asserted in accordance with section 77 of the Copyright, Designs and Patents Act 1988.

This book is in copyright. Subject to statutory exception and to provisions of relevant collective licensing agreements, no reproduction of any part may take place without the written permission of Influx Press.

This edition 2025
Printed and bound in the UK by Clays
Paperback ISBN: 9781914391507
Ebook ISBN: 9781914391514

Cover design: Luke Bird
Text design: Sean Preston
Editor: Gary Budden
Proofreader: Fleur Tizard

This book is sold subject to the condition that it shall not, by way of trade or otherwise, be lent, re-sold, hired out, or otherwise circulated without the publisher's prior consent in any form of binding or cover other than that in which it is published and without a similar condition including this condition being imposed on the subsequent purchaser.

This is a work of fiction. Unless otherwise indicated, all the names, characters, businesses, places, events and incidents in this book are either the product of the author's imagination or used in a fictitious manner. Any resemblance to actual persons, living or dead, or actual events is purely coincidental.

**Praise for *Deliverywoman***

'I love a short story collection in which the author holds distinct moments up to examine them from different angles, letting the light hit them just so. This is what Eva Wyles does in *Deliverywoman* – life is shown to us by sometimes strange characters in often compelling settings. We are thrown into odd spaces where the rules are different from the everyday, though everything feels familiar, and we realise that, yes, life is absurd and it's hard to figure out what to do next. Yet we have these companions, and the promise of a few good stories, brought together by a gifted writer, to keep us company.'
— Tina Makereti, author of *The Mires*

'These compelling, acutely observed stories examine the points at which lives intersect. Characters connect and exit: passing each other, colliding, departing. They navigate their way through the heat of beginnings and endings, and try to make sense of everything in between.'
— Anna Taylor, author of *Relief*

'There is a beautiful anthropology to Wyles' writing; these are stories that know what makes us tick before we do.'
— Leah Dodd, author of *Past Lives*

'*Deliverywoman* builds a world that is both familiar and unfamiliar. Stories of debaucherous ski fields and summer house parties lead into stories of a desolate, post-pandemic future: where the streets are mostly empty and connection is fraught. These characters are lonely and often lost, but each story leaves you feeling that hope is just around the corner.'
— Joy Holley, author of *Dream Girls*

*To my parents*

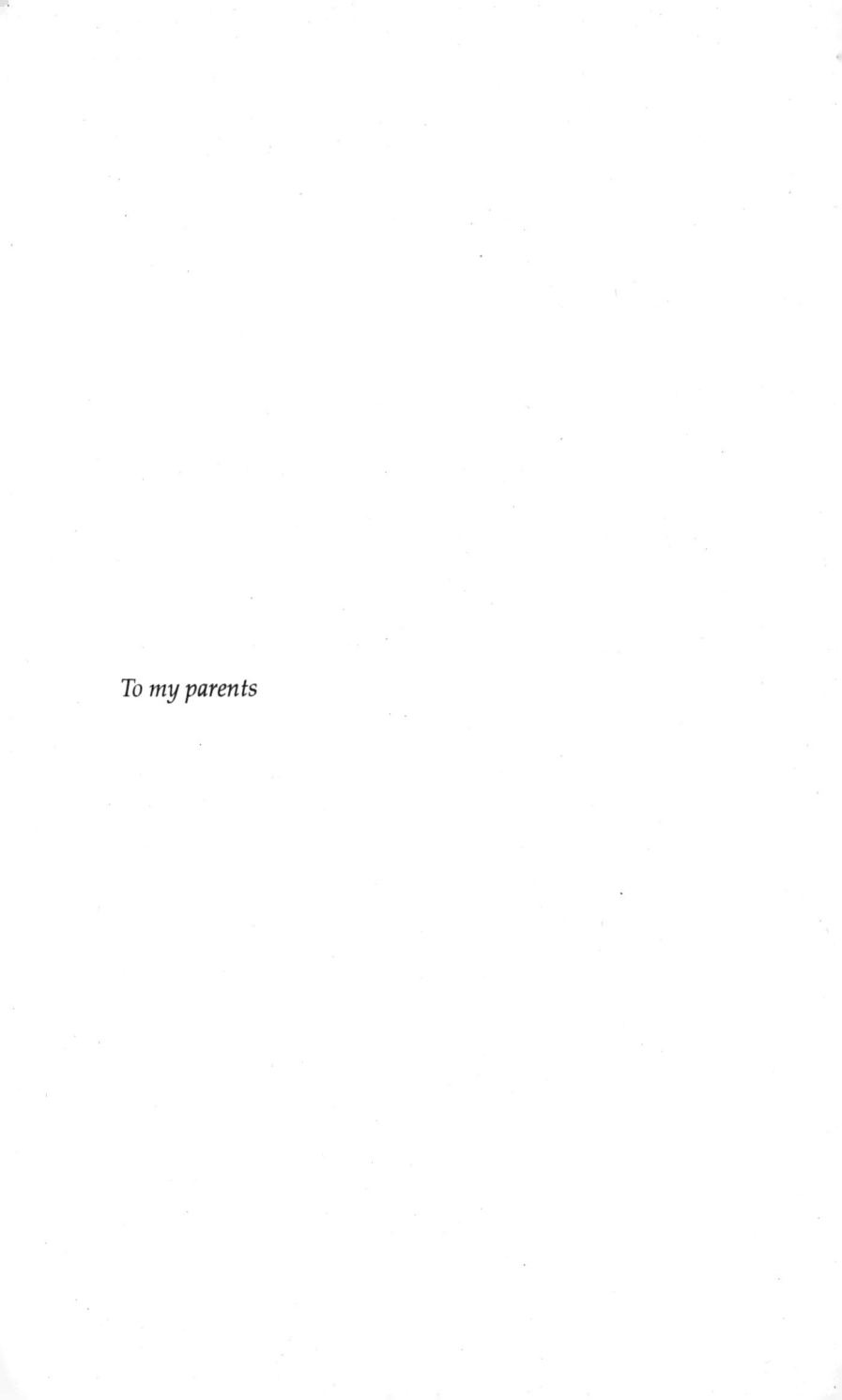

# CONTENTS

| | |
|---|---|
| Mother And | 13 |
| A Little Mess | 21 |
| So, Sorry | 31 |
| Good Boy | 45 |
| Bad Kid | 81 |
| It Waits | 93 |
| Simon Eagle | 115 |
| Twinning | 127 |
| Familial Reunions | 151 |
| Two Women, Swinging | 175 |
| Dave | 191 |
| Painting Work | 211 |
| Deliverywoman | 233 |

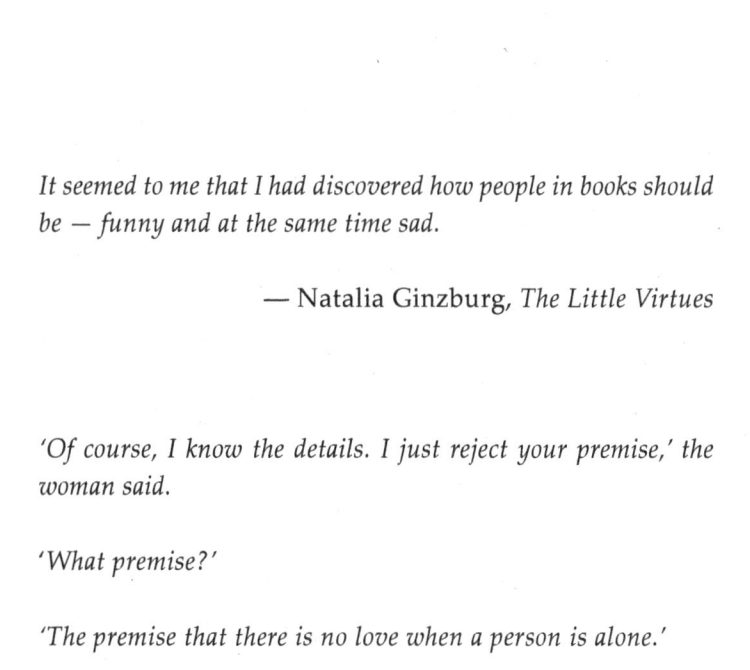

*It seemed to me that I had discovered how people in books should be — funny and at the same time sad.*

— Natalia Ginzburg, *The Little Virtues*

*'Of course, I know the details. I just reject your premise,' the woman said.*

*'What premise?'*

*'The premise that there is no love when a person is alone.'*

— Hilary Leichter, *Terrace Story*

# MOTHER AND

'Time I went,' uttered the woman, then paused to look over her shoulder. The old man had been there since she'd arrived, on the opposite end of the pontoon, looking towards the blue horizon with his legs half sunk in the sea. They had never met before, but despite this, had enjoyed, or so she hoped, a few moments of boundless peace with one another. The woman spoke again. 'Have a funeral to attend,' she said.

When no response was given, she used her hands to lift her bottom off the wet wood and plonk her body underwater. Then she was underwater with her eyes closed. Then she was above water with her eyes open. Then she was on the shore, looking back at the man. The woman thought about yelling across the ocean between them, something like 'only trying to make conversation!' but then wondered whether he may be deaf, or grieving, or anything else that would excuse him of being rude and give the label over to her instead. Lifting a towel above her waist, the woman began to both undress and dress, so that only her feet remained bare while she zig-zagged up the path back home.

Her husband was sitting at the dining table when she arrived. Her son was leaning on the porch steps, lacing up his shoes. The old man was still on the pontoon, but the distance had taken his age away and left him with only a silhouette. The woman brushed her feet off, shedding sand, and laughed. She had learnt – over the years – to laugh at herself before others got the chance.

'Talking to strangers again?' said her son.

'Hardly.' She sat down on the step with him and sighed.

'Sighing again,' he said.

'And why is it that you think I'm sighing all the time?'

The son sighed too. 'Because of your expectations,' he replied. Behind them, her husband sighed himself, before typing something out on his keyboard. The woman raised her eyebrows. Her son went on. 'The whole world is filled with people expecting some kind of moment to appear. Which it never does. Or if it does, they expect another after that. Hence disappointment. Hence sighing.' He stretched out so that his feet dangled off the final step. 'You talk to strangers in case something great might happen.'

'I talk to strangers to be friendly.'

'But what are you hoping to get from being friendly?'

The woman leant over and fondly tousled his hair. 'The world does not always work that way.'

The boy shrugged her away and began to reorganise his curls. 'It does,' he replied. 'You just need to answer honestly.'

When he had researched, analysed, and decided upon the rules of the world, she did not know.

He looked out across the bay. 'What time is Mary's service?'

The woman checked her watch. 'Ten minutes. Will you still join? We could go for a swim afterwards.'

'You just went swimming,' he stated, and stood up, revealing his long, almost-hairy legs. 'Okay,' he said. 'But I have to go see Josh afterwards, so no swim.'

A row of heads bobbed on the screen. Some had familiar haircuts, a bush of red pinned together that the woman knew well, while others could just as well have belonged to the bodies of people she might pass on a busy street, or aboard a bus. There was a chorus of hushed whispers, and every so often, the pastor testing the microphone. It was a church neither of them had set foot in before, and the woman found herself looking for details so as to build an image in her head that she could sit in. There was a line of four mosaicked windows, a small wooden stage with a lectern, two stands with vases holding plastic bouquets, a sloped ceiling with a hanging projector displaying images of Mary, and what appeared to be a young IT assistant, perched at the piano bench, bent over and untangling a thick coil of wires.

The son lightly elbowed the woman. 'It's you,' he said.

He was right. On the projector was a photograph of Mary and three others, the woman included, in their swimsuits and caps on the nearby wharf, with their wide happy legs poised to jump.

'Oh, it used to be so cold,' the woman began. 'But we did it—'

'Every week,' the son finished.

The image slid away and was replaced by another – this one showing Mary in bed, connected to an array of machines, smiling and holding a newborn baby, her nephew, up for the camera to see. Feet on wooden steps came through the computer speaker, and there was a light hush as the audience quietened.

'We are here today to show our love and support for Mary's friends and family,' the pastor began. 'Who loved her so dearly through her life, and will continue to do so, even now that she is no longer with us.'

The woman could not help but train her eyes on the IT assistant. Still seated at the piano bench, small patches of sweat had begun to darken his grey shirt at the join, and his own eyes, barely visible through the screen, appeared to be darting between the wires and the projector screen, where a black line had made its way across the images.

'I will keep this short as family and friends intend to share their personal stories of times with Mary. Gus, Mary's husband, will speak first, followed by Jean, Mary's twin sister, and then Pauline, Mary's closest friend. What I would like to say, in brief, is a note on grief.'

The IT assistant dragged a spindly hand through his hair as the black line flashed and the projector went completely blank. Mary's sister, a tall woman, made her way to where he was seated, and began to speak behind a closed hand while he nodded profusely.

'What's happening?' the son said, and the woman lightly lifted her shoulders before dropping them back down again.

'Today and tomorrow and the day after that, you will grieve the loss of Mary,' the pastor continued. 'And learn to live a life without Mary – whom I've learnt was a ray of sunshine in your lives. Your hearts will draw together and extend in what is to come, in a way you never thought possible, for the human heart knows no bounds to pain, and we see it break and carry on through our own living lives, limitlessly.'

Mary's sister was bent down, her own arms inside the bundle of wires now.

'In the coming times, remember Mary for the good that she brought you. The sort of good that is complicated, I'm sure, in the way all humans are. But, in the face of all that grief, remember how magical it can be to meet another human and hold space in your hearts for one another. That does not need to go away now that Mary is no longer here. She can still live in your hearts.'

Mary's sister rammed a plug into a socket, and the images returned, this one showing an image of Mary and her toddler at the time, standing on the shore's edge with a small wave collapsing against their ankles.

The woman and the son listened in silence as different people ascended and descended the stage to speak. Some spoke directly to the audience while others lowered their heads in the direction of notes. Every so often, the woman sniffed her nose, or stretched her hand out and ran it down her thigh.

When the service was over and the in-person attendees were invited to move into the reception room for afternoon tea, the woman and the son remained seated. They watched in resolute silence as people stood and milled about, hugging, and then as the clusters eventually moved away, the son stood. The woman looked up at him, how tall he'd gotten, and then stood too. He leant down and put his arms around her. 'That was beautiful, Mum,' he said, and as their hug withdrew, he put his hand on her shoulder and gave it a light squeeze.

The old man was nowhere to be seen when she returned to the beach. School kids circled the pontoon, taking turns climbing aboard and jumping off. The woman took her shirt off and waded in. Once she was halfway submerged, she was able to make out the wharf where they used to jump off with Mary the previous year. The woman had not been there since that summer. At the pontoon, she did not talk, nor did she climb the ladder and sit, but instead swam around it and returned to shore.

She did not know why she returned to the home office after her second swim. To her muted surprise, she had forgotten to exit the window and the service was still being streamed, only the guests had long departed, leaving behind a single cleaner, who looked remarkably similar to the IT assistant, only older, tugging a vacuum cleaner around the floor with a long winding cord. The woman also did not know why she sat back down and watched as the cleaner moved between his tasks: unpinning photographs of Mary from the cork board, collecting discarded funeral programmes, stacking seats, clearing the stage, taking out the rubbish bags. He was consistent with his speed, quiet in his gestures, and not once did he make eye contact with the screen. Twenty, thirty, forty minutes passed. Sounds of the husband departing floated in – a clearing of plates, a closing of his own laptop, a goodbye call. Outside, the gate clicked closed. A rubbish truck lifted bottles into its bowels and let the glass smash. The woman watched as the cleaner pressed his foot down on the vacuum and the cord shot back inside the barrel, wheeling it out of view, leaving behind the emptied church, stripped of evidence from the previous service and ready for the next.

# A LITTLE MESS

The first thing George did when he arrived at work was splash his face with water. There was something about the white-white light inside that made him feel immediately dirty. Not to mention the bathroom, no matter how many times they sterilised it, always felt like it was awash with sticky piss. He'd recently asked for the morning shifts, because even though they cleaned the petrol station at four-hour intervals, he felt that the morning customers surely had to have tidier tendencies than the ones at night.

At home, in his parents' garage, everything was neat. Sometimes, when he was lying in bed, George thought he could hear his parents standing in the overgrown garden, talking about him – murmurs of him getting a girlfriend, them finally being grandparents, he was thirty after all, wasn't it time for him to move out?

'Morning G-man,' Alistair said without looking up from the till computer.

'Morning A-man.'

Alistair smirked, still not looking up. 'Bro, you gotta stop that, A-man doesn't work.'

'Alright,' George lifted his hands in surrender. 'What's on the agenda this morning?'

'First up, I'd like you to get ready to destroy the world. It's probably a good idea to look yourself in the mirror and say *it's time to fuck this shit up*. Then go stand outside and wait for any old geezer to pull up so you can offer them a hand in filling their hunk of metal with death liquid.'

Alistair did this most mornings – he was younger and more inclined to joke about the painfully true parts of the job. Afterwards, he usually looked up to check if he'd gained a reaction, which George always dutifully gave in the form of a smile, before snapping back into the platitudes of their morning routine.

'Actual though, I gotta do this online training thing so you may as well restock the pie ovens. Think we're running low on steak.'

George had a look around the store floor. There was a packet of Doritos lying on its side in the chip aisle, and something about the rows of chocolate bars looked wrong to him. Maybe the Twixes were more to the left than usual. 'Done the bathroom yet?' he asked.

'Na, not yet,' Alistair replied. He was always late on the bathroom cleanups.

'Okay, I'll just give it a spritz and then get onto the pies.'

'Why you gotta be so anal about the bathroom?' Alistair joked.

'People are disgusting,' George replied.

## A LITTLE MESS

Through the swinging door, George snapped on a pair of rubber gloves and began to spray disinfectant around the sink while he waited for the water to run hot. Then, he tilted a bucket under the tap and swirled it around with some bleach, before dumping it on the floor. He pushed the mop in persistent motions around the tiles, letting the suds settle into the grooves before squeezing residue back into the bucket. With every movement, he felt cleaner, more capable.

When he re-entered the store, a woman was standing by the shelves of oil. She looked familiar to him, something about her hair. She was sipping on a carton of strawberry milk. Alistair was nowhere to be found, so George went to stand behind the counter, where he stole glances at her while pretending to look at something on the computer screen. It was as if she'd been to Bluff and back, the way her face felt to watch. As though she knew something no one else did. Like the beauty of the country's cold toes. George had never been to Bluff, never even made it past Nelson. Apart from her face, she was dressed the way he expected a Lyall Bayer to dress, only her hair was a little purple at the ends, like a Newtowner. Probably a Berhamporer, George thought to himself, and looked out the window in time to catch Alistair putting out a cigarette.

'Hello.' She'd walked up to the counter without making a peep.

'Hi.'

'I've got no idea what sort of oil I'm supposed to put in my car.' She looked over his shoulder as she took another sip of milk. 'Think I could bother you for some help?'

As he walked over to the shelves, being careful not to move too quickly, he caught a whiff of her. She smelt of something he couldn't place – like wet mud, or wool.

'What type of car have you got?' he asked.

'Uhhh, that one,' she said, pointing through the window at a beaten-up Toyota.

'Manual or auto?'

'Auto.'

'This one should do the trick,' he mumbled, picking up a black bottle with an electric red label. 'Works on any general auto.'

'Thanks,' she smiled. After paying, she said thanks again, then walked outside.

He turned to the computer, registering the screen properly this time. Alistair's module was still up, sitting on the question:

*What is the first thing you do if someone in-store becomes violent?*

A) *Politely ask them to leave.*

B) *Tell them you're going to call the police.*

C) *Press the red button which calls the police.*

D) *All of the above.*

'Stupid, isn't it?' Alistair said as he joined George at the counter. 'Like I'm going to do anything except tell them to fuck off?'

'What are we meant to do?' George replied genuinely.

'Probably A and B and C.'

'So D?'

'Yeah. Click it for me, will you?'

George clicked D and a green tick appeared.

'Nice,' Alistair said. 'I'm gonna take a dump real quick, mind doing the next question for me?'

Alistair walked away before George had time to reply. George looked out the window. The Berhamporer was still there, peering into her engine, holding the bonnet up with her left hand. Maybe I should go and hold it for her, George thought. Be a gentleman. Maybe she would flirt with him and maybe he would flirt back. Maybe they would get a drink together. She'd become his girlfriend. Tell his parents. Have a baby. Everyone would be happy. But then again, she would never flirt with him, George thought. Why would she? He clicked 'next'.

*Where is the first aid kit stored?*

A)   *The cleaning supplies cupboard.*

B)   *Beneath the cigarettes cabinet.*

B)   *Underneath the cash register.*

C)   *None of the above.*

Next to each of the options was a picture. George clicked on the image of the shelving beneath the register, where they also kept the spare uniforms. Another green tick appeared.

'Sorry to bother you again, but you just look so familiar.' It was the Berhamporer speaking. She was back in the store, this time holding a vape instead of a milk carton. 'Is there any chance your name is George?'

'Yes,' he said. 'Sorry—'

'It's Polly. You might not remember me; we went to school togeth—'

'Polly. Polly? Polly Croft?' George blurted.

'Yeah,' she beamed. 'I can't believe it's actually you.'

Polly had been one of the few people from their primary school that had actually gone somewhere overseas. Australia, or England, George thought. In school, she'd teased him for eating lunch alone, then asked whether he wanted to sit with her. He'd ignored the latter and felt strange about eating lunch alone ever since, though he failed to make the connection between that incident and all the lunches that followed. Even when it was sunny, he chose to eat his packed lunches inside with whoever was on shift with him.

'How have you been?' he asked.

'Oh, good. How have you been?' she replied.

'I've been good.'

'That's good.'

They stood in silence. While she flipped her vape over in her hand, George thought about what his friend, Jonny, had said to him the weekend before. *Girls are like parrots, you've got to sing to them to get them to sing back.* They'd been sitting at a pub. George had shuddered. To him, there was nothing worse than drunkenly discussing how to get women when it was clear they were the most undesirable men there.

Alistair walked back into the store. 'Ahoy there.'

Polly turned around, tucked her hair behind her ears.

'Good trip?' George asked.

'Bloody brilliant. All sorted here?' Alistair waggled his index finger between George and Polly.

'Yep,' George said quickly.

'Actually,' Polly turned back to George. 'I was wondering whether you could help me with that oil? I think I've poured it into the wrong hole.' She pulled her lips back to make a zipped expression with her teeth.

'Sure,' George replied.

Outside, the wind had started to pick up. The two Pōhutukawa trees at the edge of the concrete forecourt creaked as they walked over to her car. Polly unlatched the bonnet and held it up, with her right hand this time. She used her left hand to point at the overflow tank. 'There, that's where I put the oil.'

George looked at her nails, which were smattered with green polish and pressed with a fine line of dirt. 'Okay, okay,' he said. 'Alright.'

'Is that bad?' she asked.

'It's not great. That's where you usually put the water.'

'Fuck,' she said, bringing one of her fingers to her mouth and nibbling on it. It made George feel sorry for her. 'I have a job interview in fifteen minutes.'

His time had finally arrived. 'It'll be okay, I have a car,' he said.

After letting Alistair know he was darting out, to which Alistair replied, 'Awoogah awoogah,' George showed Polly to his own, slightly cleaner, Toyota. They drove past the needle sculpture tipping in the wind, through the tunnel of honks, all the way into the city where they proceeded to stop bluntly at a series of STOP signs.

'You were so quiet in school,' she said, as if talking to no one in particular.

'I guess I still am.'

'I think I've just gotten quieter,' Polly said. She took an inhale of her vape. 'Shit, sorry. I default smoke around people I know.' She rolled the window down.

'It's okay, smoke away.'

She put the vape back into her bag anyway.

'How come you've gotten quieter?' He turned down a one-way street.

'Oh, I don't know. I probably just used to be too loud. Scared everyone away.'

'Hardly.'

'I scared you!' she laughed. 'I remember telling my ma I wanted to be your friend. That's a bit embarrassing to say, isn't it? But it's true.'

'Really?'

'Truly.'

She got out at the next set of lights, running off in the direction of Featherston Street. 'See you when I get my shit together and pick up that car…' her voice trailed off behind her. George watched as she disappeared behind a corner. He looked left and right before bringing the car back around in a

## A LITTLE MESS

U-turn. By the time he'd returned to the petrol station, he'd decided to get his shit together, too. He wasn't sure if he meant it yet. The first thing he did when he was back inside was go stand in the bathroom. Instead of looking at the grime, he peered at himself in the mirror and tried to smile. He could hear Alistair singing along to the radio. Something about sticking with it. George went to look at the rows of chocolate bars. He'd been right, the Twixes were usually where the Moros were – the price stickers were mixed up too. George thought about fixing it. He tried to tell himself a little mess was okay, then started switching them over anyway. Twix, Moro, Twix, Moro. No, stop it, he told himself, and started moving them back to the wrong positions.

# SO, SORRY

Dear Margot,

Know you're probably thinking, who the hell! Fifteen years no contact and then, a letter! Anyway, hi. Am writing to you because I have reached a point of crisis, and have wanted to apologise to you for some time. When I look back on when it began (the crisis), your face comes to mind. Not that I'm blaming you – it is more like the essence of your face is there. I think the crisis is because I'm lonely, or drinking too much, or not sleeping enough, and then it dissipates, and the freckles on your face emerge. Just, well, it took me a long time to realise that the day I turned my back on you was the first time I felt a centimetre of air between myself and the ground beneath me.

So, sorry. So sorry. Do you remember, when we were ten, and we started our Silly Club? We made those certificates with ClipArt monkeys on them and awarded them to the silliest member that week. And remember how, on Tuesdays, we would meet by the oak tree to deliberate? Arguing about whether Tom who pulled his pants down in maths or Jackie who stuck Mr. Wilson's prized sticker collection across the girls' toilet cubicles deserved the certificate more. I think about it. Lately, I think about it often.

Got to say I miss you, even though I barely know you now. But do you believe that maybe inside everyone there is a small glowing parcel of being that never changes? That if you and I were to find ourselves in a room together, we might be able to find those parcels and let them visit each other, even if just for a moment?

I can still stalk you from up here, even though you don't post that much. A picture of the sky, or your children (they are so cute!) and I start wondering who you are behind it all – whether you too find yourself with a shadow-self trailing you. Mine is over 80 million kilometres away. If you and I had known that when we were children, deciding who to award the certificate to, we would have had a right giggle. And we probably would have broken our rule of not awarding ourselves certificates, being the Presidents of the club and all, and written my name down. Because how I've lived my life is by far the silliest, and yet, not the least bit funny.

Or maybe you find it funny. Maybe, when you're feeding your children their breakfast and one of them is having a tantrum, maybe, just maybe, you think to yourself God, what a hoot that Emily became such a star. Or maybe, when you and your husband (you never post pictures of him – why?) are watching a TV show together you think to yourself, it is just so weirdly hilarious that I used to be friends with Emily Shapel. I still remember when you said, on our way to high school, that I had a famous person's name. Maybe after all this, I should blame you. Now wouldn't that be silly.

If you will let me (not that you can consent immediately, given this is *off*line, so I'm going to keep on writing, and if you'd like to stop reading, just stop), I'm going to tell you what happened, from my point of view. Then, if you're in the mood to reply, maybe you can do the same. And then, it will at least all be shared. This silence has been so wide and long – I often wonder whether it has taken more from my life than it has given. Because nothing – nothing – has come close to filling the silence between us. God, it sounds like I'm making this into such a massive deal. Which I guess it is, for me. But you're probably going to be standing at your letterbox, a normal day either starting or finishing, zero premonition within you that something like this (dramatic?) is coming. So, sorry if that is the case.

Wonder if you remember me as someone that used to babble. I certainly do.

Like most childhood friendships, it just happened. Somewhere between learning to count and learning to write we agreed to a coalition. It is funny, now, to think of how children are capable of this. We were learning to sing the alphabet and then we were promising one another everything. It was incredible your Mum was so happy to have me over all the time – as if it were easy to feed, transport, and care for another child. I loved your Mum, I'm so sorry.

I want to assure you it was also not a simple case of my seeking out a friend with a Motherly Mum to replace my own. She was a Motherly Mum to me because you were her child. When I'm asked the question, 'Describe your childhood?', (it has become low hanging fruit due to a number of exposés on my childhood I have regretfully read), it is you that I think about. It is the way you carefully climbed trees, and how you often took your shoes and socks off to get a better grip. It is the year our baby teeth started falling out. You must have told your Mum because I woke up with a note from the tooth fairy beneath my pillow. It is all the imaginary games we played. It is how, as we grew up – became twelve, thirteen, fourteen – and stopped having as many sleepovers, you still called most nights because you knew I had trouble sleeping. Do you remember when we used to count down before hanging up? Whispering *on three? One. I love you. Two. I love you. Three. I love you.*

This is where it gets hard, because I'm going to continue to write from my point of view, fully aware of how cruel it must have been, to you. I must admit I'm questioning whether this is the most appropriate route to be taking. I suppose I want you to understand that success has not been as great as it may have seemed. My life has been tainted with regret, and the only feasible way I can think of explaining this is by laying the details out for you to judge, and hoping you might, in turn, tell me about yours.

So, well, here you go. About halfway through the school term, when I was sitting in the school corridor, I was approached by a group of girls (you know the ones) because I had apparently become pretty. I'm still not sure where you were at the time, or why I was alone, but I remember feeling like I was on the edge of something. An argument with my Mum, or something hormonal, and then they were standing there, in front of me, asking whether I wanted to eat lunch with them. For the first time in my life, I felt highly visible, like I had just been stamped into opacity. You and I had lived in our own special world until then. The whole thing was truly plucked straight from a stupid film, and it was scary. I went with them. The entirety of that lunchtime was terrifying – watching them pass around comments and laughter. But in the same stroke, it felt good to be someone. For so long, I had only been someone to you.

I told you about it after school and we laughed in that way where we weren't really sure what it was we were laughing at. I remember it clearly – we were sitting on the football field and it was cloudy. It sounded like your laugh was directed at their audacity to offer their invitations, and mine sounded like I was baffled at their thinking I was worthy of one. We exchanged remarks that didn't quite connect with the others – avoiding the real question at hand, which I suppose was whether I would see them again. We never did ask or answer the question, but I recall there being something in the way we said goodbye that day, a look in your eyes that was equally searching and caring, as if you were wishing me safe travels on where I was about to go.

The group of girls were remarkably persistent (if memory testifies), and I gave in (or dutifully submitted). I had full autonomy, but I guess I was young. It always seems to go that way – people push the blame onto themselves, then others, then bring it back on themselves.

Blame likes to shoot around, doesn't it? Soon enough, they'd become my friends. And with it, a whole new way of—

God, I hate writing this stuff down. It is so... blah blah. Woe me for becoming pretty and benefiting from it. But honestly, I suppose it is one of my greatest regrets. Because that was the beginning of the beginning of it all. Only a month later, your Mum passed. I know I do not need to remind you of that. I will never be able to understand how it all happened.

How she was there, and then she wasn't.

Then, you went away. First, in the non-physical sense, drifting between classrooms. I still remember trying to wave you over to where I was, and it happens in slow motion in my memory, but you looked over, nodded, and it was as if that was goodbye. Then you left, in the very physical sense, a few weeks later. You moved in with your aunt in Beckenham. I don't have a clue how you managed everything you did. The grief. Months went by. I wrote you a couple of letters, omitting any mention of my further indoctrination into the group, but soon put them into hibernation without ever taking them to the post office. I don't remember much else from that time, except for how disconnected I felt from whoever I had once been. It's hard to make any sense of how I was with you. I missed you, but it was like I couldn't access it. In its place, instead, was everything the group taught me about what I could control, which was my appearance. I learned how to lose weight using the harshest methods, and sat in the sun whenever I could – so much so that I'm surprised I haven't gotten skin cancer. I spent hours, hours, studying pictures of myself.

The thing is, it wasn't all awful (there is a sort of beauty in all social compositions). I became very close with some of them – Issy in particular. And our friendship was loving, in its own way. We would spend hours talking about parties and boys, but we would still find ourselves up against the existential. No matter how popular you are, that cloud of thought still manages to visit. But through those clouds, we became close. Comrades, like a team. We knew how to help the other avoid whatever storm was passing, how to help the other dress in a way that felt simultaneously comfortable and appealing to others, how to make each other laugh, even if it was at someone's expense.

Then, the following year, you returned. And you seemed to have gone off in an entirely different direction. Your hair was light red. I'm not sure why that detail is important, but I suppose I remember your head resurfacing along the edge of the school gates, and I was standing nearby, so focussed on what Issy was telling me about a horrible argument she'd had with her dad that I didn't look properly. A head of red, bobbing, then you turned a corner, and there you were. Your face, body, parcel soul, back inside the school gates. And I turned away, before you could see me. Led Issy somewhere out of sight so we could continue our conversation.

You didn't come back to school – you were only there to sign the exit papers. There was only six months left, and you started working at a supermarket. You texted, once, saying you wanted to see me, and then I saw a video of you at a party falling down some stairs, and I never replied.

That's when it started – I was standing at a dingy bar we'd used fake IDs to get into, and Issy showed me the video, laughing, and said, 'Didn't you used to be friends with her?' and I laughed back and said, 'Yeah, jeez,' and up I went. Just a smidge – but I could no longer feel the ground beneath me. I wedged my index finger under my shoe to check, and sure enough, I could get a tip in without too much trouble.

After that, well. I feel like I'm recapping without explaining why I did such things. And this is probably because I myself don't understand. It was like I had no choice. Like some societal god or reputational guru had decided that was what I should do. Which is probably the opposite of religion.

You let me go quietly. One or two more messages, a couple of awkward run-ins, and you stopped trying. I don't know how you managed. Not in the way that I imagine you missed me, but in the way that you were probably confronted with the incalculable fact that you had been friends with someone so shallow.


The cliché continued. I got into modelling. Ha, ha. I didn't even know such a job existed when we were friends. It was Issy who showed me how to walk and how to pose, and we spent a few years doing it together before she stopped getting jobs and moved onto low budget acting. When I signed with an agency and started to travel for work, Issy and I kept in touch for a year or so before resigning to the kind of contact acquaintances keep – wishing one another happy birthday, or liking a post. I don't know what or who she is today, apart from the fact she eventually moved back home (do you see her around?) and has a dog named Cleo.

For the next few years, my days were made up of simple tasks. I would exercise, have an occasional photoshoot, do a social activity that would also be photographed, and spend my free time poring over how I looked in mirrors or phone cameras. I quite happily forgot about any other characteristics pertaining to a personality. I'd like to say it was exhausting, but in reality, it was the most straightforward my life has ever been. Sure, it pained me on the days I loathed how I looked. But the majority of the time I was swallowed by a singular, seemingly manageable, goal.

I made some new friends and dated a few good-looking, vapid guys in between. Sometimes they would make me laugh, but most of the time the people I kept company with served a purpose – they were there to reinforce the image I had of myself. Never did I feel the same kind of love I felt for you – the kind where I loved that parcel of being inside of them.

And each time I stepped further into this life, the gap between myself and the ground grew some more.

Actually, if I think about it, it wasn't stepping into this life that did it. Really, it was every time I had a chance to do something good for myself or for others, even something as small as having a genuine conversation, and chose to do the wrong thing so I could get a step further in notoriety. You are probably well aware of the mechanisms of fame – or at least the understanding that nothing will ever be enough. Why else would celebrities become super-celebrities? Why else do super-celebrities continue to go higher?

So, up and up I went. At first, like I said, the space grew in smidges. Then I think a certain crescendo moment was reached. There was no going back, I mean. Sure, sometimes I'd go back down to Earth for a moment – to cry when something didn't go my way, or to take my make-up off, or to sleep. But these moments always felt very afraid of themselves, ready to be snapped shut like a pocket mirror. It was easier to keep going; the alternative was too difficult. And it became a sort of game, and aren't players of games the best at avoiding love? I took myself beyond anything I could have ever imagined. I was on billboards and catwalks and couldn't go a day without spying myself caressing a bottle of perfume with fingers so airbrushed I barely recognised them as my own.

The strangest thing – how everything flew up with me. Well, not everything, just the things pertaining to my status. In the early days, when I found myself at the level of regular ceiling height, I could only interact with the people also deemed to be of ceiling height status. Issy was there with me, but no one else from the group. We had plenty to do up there – cocktail bars and Ubers and pretty good parties in nicely decorated apartments.

Then, when I began travelling for work, and reached the stratosphere, the only people I could interact with were people of moderate fame – probably C-list, if you wanted to try and grade it. I didn't mind – we were still in the business of helping one another have a good time. We'd take pictures together and snort lines – all the things people probably imagine we do – and get a little higher, mentally and physically. During the day, I'd go to sessions with a personal trainer and sit in expensive cafés. I bought my first house in the stratosphere. At a certain point, maybe in the mesosphere, I remember feeling a pang for connection. It is a human need, after all. But I'd successfully estranged myself from Mum, and no longer talked to anyone I'd once had a vague sense of connection with, and so decided to look for it around me.

That was how I met Dan, crazy Dan. He had greasy hair that went halfway down his back and starred in all kinds of outrageous movies involving pirates and the galaxy. The thing I liked about him most was that he did his own stunts. I think I thought it was very real of him. Anyway, he and I shared some form of love, for a time. We even decided to move in together in a high-ceilinged studio on the edge of the thermosphere. A year went by. We fought, we cheated on one another, we made up. Mostly, I remember feeling useless. I have this memory that doesn't belong to a time because it happened so often. In it, I am sitting at the kitchen island alone. I have a drink in my hand, and Dan is outside by the pool. We have guests around. I can hear everyone else's conversation. Everyone wants to be *in* my company, but nobody wants my company.


It's such a strange sensation to know the whole world is watching you, and yet your lives become so insular, in a way. Your image becomes available to everyone, and the population of people you can actually talk to completely shrinks. There are no meandering conversations about which flowers smell the nicest or someone foreign coming up to you and asking if you know how to get from A to B. Some people do find fame without flying so high – I'll admit the fault is partially my own with how far I've gone. They come from large families that stabilise them in the stratosphere, or engage in ordinary activities with ordinary people, sometimes so much so they've never even departed Earth. I used to think this was a sign they had failed. Now, I see it's the opposite. Dan and I split, unsurprisingly, and I actually flew higher after it was made public. I'm honestly not sure how far up you can go, but I can see planets where I am.

I wonder what you can see? Maybe it's your steering wheel because you're driving somewhere. Or maybe it's a computer screen because you're reading something online, or maybe you stay offline, and you're reading a newspaper? Maybe someone has just knocked on the door, a meter reader or a plumber, and you're asking them if they'd like a cup of tea. Or maybe you're asleep, and you're watching the back of your eyelids as though they're a movie screen, and dreams of the ocean and your children and overdue chores are swirling together. That all sounds so nice. It has become so quiet up here. There is barely anyone around. And, well, with all this time alone, I've started thinking again. And I'm thinking – I haven't lived in so long. It's so lonely up here. And I'm so sorry, to you and to myself, for creating such a ginormous distance between us.

So, well, I guess what I'm trying to say is, I wish I could do ordinary things with you. I wish I also had children and a house and a regular job and I'd figured out a way to enjoy

## SO, SORRY

life's daily mundanities. I imagine you making dinner for your daughter, cutting up carrots, dicing onions, looking out the window at a garden you think needs more work. I sometimes try to imagine myself in the same elemental sort of way – putting gas in the car, or feeding chickens, or watching the silhouettes of trees fall across a lawn. Maybe in an alternate universe we would call one another up and talk to each other about these things, or sit on your porch and have a glass of wine and laugh again. I wish I could witness these things instead of imagining them. The carrots, the chickens, the friendship. But I worry I have been filled up with so much of the extreme, that even if given the chance, I could never look at them the way you might be able to.

So, I might wrap this up here. Not too sure where it's going, or where I'm going. I'm not expecting you to fix any of this, just to say I'm sorry I haven't gotten in touch earlier, and that our friendship meant a lot to me. And that I'm glad – as horrible as it sounds – that you are not up here with me, because it means you must be much closer to your shadow shelf than I am to mine.

With love,

Emily

# GOOD BOY

I arrived in Drift as I did each Winter – a little unsure of myself, a bit careless, barely curious. The narrow overhead compartments of the bus were full when I'd boarded in Vancouver, and so I'd spent the majority of the journey with my sports bag at my feet, backpack on my knees, same as the person next to me – like a can of SEAT 42A and SEAT 42B sardines. When we pulled into the outskirts of Drift, I got that familiar tingle in my chest at the sight of all the excitable tourists standing outside the equipment rental stores, local kids let loose on Glen Street, weary old women pushing trolleys around the Driftside Market car park. The two populations of the town amused me. You don't get those extremes mingling much place else. Bigger the city, easier the separation. But here you had the richest of the rich and the poorest of the poor, and they all acted as if they owned the place. I liked playing poor when I got there. To be fair, I was doing a poor man's job, slopping food into bowls, washing down industrial sized trays, but I was getting paid twice as much as any local in the township, simply because I was higher up on the mountain.

---

Back home, I often spent my days alone. Kept this old job my stepmother sorted me in secondary school where I listened to recordings of therapy sessions and wrote notes for the psychiatrist. Horrible stuff. Sexual abuse, emotional abuse, physical abuse, domestic abuse, as well as the regular complaints about work or relationships or both, revelations on the way they were going to start living their life now that they had cracked the latest life motto! Et cetera, et cetera. My boyfriend, Xavier, often told people I was a freelancer when they asked him what I did for work. I don't blame him – I often made it sound a lot more consuming than it was. We lived together, but he worked in an office full time as some kind of executive assistant. I never did know exactly what he did on an hourly basis, just that he was always stressed. Anyway, by the time I surfaced in the morning he'd have left long before me, leaving behind small traces of his carefully spent morning – tucking the sheets in on his side of the bed, a half pot of coffee for me (I never did tell him it was cold by the time I got to it), tidying the cushions on the sofa, and sometimes even a small note wishing me some kind of good day. It was normally midday by the time I got in the shower. Depending on my mood I'd either microwave the cold coffee or make another pot. Shower and the rest, eventually slump into the couch to do three or four hours of listening and typing, then start making dinner. Tell Xavier I went to the library, what a big day I just had.

Drift was my time to really live. It was the only place I enjoyed being forced to get up early, shaken alive by the orchestra of other people's alarms and being thrust into minimum -21°C temperatures for my 5:00am shift. Something in the icy air molecules made it feel like I was being pumped with cocaine. And then there was the actual cocaine. Work hard, play hard. Et cetera, et cetera.

Xavier and I had been dating for eight years by the time I arrived in Drift this time around. During our first year in love, I hadn't yet discovered my need to go away. It wasn't till the third year of our relationship that a new friend of mine, Toad, suggested I join him for a season in Drift. God, we had fun together that winter. Toad knew how to party more than anyone I'd ever met. His thin wiry body was filled with electricity and an immense need for booze. We'd party all night, like all night, collecting friends and ridiculous stories along the way, getting home so drunk that we'd vomit out the window, pass out fully clothed, droplets of spew dotting our shirts, sleep for fifteen minutes, twenty if we were lucky, to find the vomit puddles were already frozen and our alarms hammering away because work was about to start. Then we'd head straight out the door, pausing every so often to keel over in the snow and puke some more. At the buffet kitchen we'd hang our aprons around our necks and giggle like school children while we exchanged whatever *remember whens* we had from the previous night, then start slicing up legs of ham as the sun began to rise over the mountain caps. The remainder of the shift would be a blur. Come 4:00pm, we'd steal what was left of the ham and munch it quickly out in the snow, then head up the chairlift and catch the last of the ski day, our bodies miraculously intact and ready to do it all again.

At that point, Xavier's and my honeymoon stage was well and truly over, and we were nestling into the ordinary parts of the relationship – criticising one another's cleaning, only ever having sex when one of us wanted to, sharing a bank account, splitting that bank account into various sub-accounts (hopeful-house, maybe-holiday, insurance, et cetera, et cetera). So, Drift was my haven. By Drift's standards, I was a clean boy. I was a nice boy. I was a good boy. Although, I will disclose that Toad and I had, one particularly coked up night, wound up fucking each other up the arse in the toilet of Dusty's, the local bar all the seasonal workers congregated at.

The following Winter, I joined Toad in Drift again, and well, the same again. It became a thing. We blitzed our way through the season with an unruly amount of substances and sex. We often talked about stopping. There were a few semi-earnest conversations right before the end of our shifts where we said things like 'this isn't fair' and 'I really like Xavier' but there was always a lack of conviction and a look beneath our presented expressions that meant whenever alcohol or drugs entered our bodies both our dicks went *ping!*

Xavier thought it was all very good of me to go off and make the amount of money I was earning, plus he said it gave him 'time to re-centre'. After the second-year fuck-fest, Toad didn't come back. He'd emailed me an uncharacteristically earnest plea for me to tell Xavier, and I told him I couldn't and wouldn't. I still wonder what his motive was for asking. Whether it was because he wanted to rid himself of the guilt or begin dating, I'm unsure. I'd still half-expected him to turn up – counting on that same lack of conviction – but it turned out he'd had some in reserve after all.

That first season without Toad, whenever I was particularly drunk, I often went to the bathroom at Dusty's with the faint feeling that he was behind me, on his way to the cubicle with me. I'm not sure what Toad does now – he almost certainly still parties, and probably spends his winters in the opposite hemisphere, somewhere sunny, perhaps surfing. Only a guess. He doesn't respond to my messages anymore. Sometimes I wonder if he'll just turn up back in Drift; not that that's why I keep coming back. It's much larger than that.

With my sports bag slung over my shoulder, I deboarded the bus, touching down in the snow and chucking a hand in the air to say thanks to the driver. I'm nothing special in the looks department – a little taller than average, brown hair, features neither captivating nor obtrusive – but I fancied myself a catch whenever I set foot in Drift. Something about the snow brought out a roguish charm in me. In the city I came off as reserved and a little antisocial, someone that spends too much time indoors. But here, a new kind of energy found its way into my bloodstream.

First thing I did was head to my accommodation. It's the same place every year, a shitty little chalet a fifteen-minute drive up the mountain. Unlike Xavier's and my apartment, it has no ulterior motive. The rooms are rooms – five of them, only two with windows. Every seat is a seat; every bed is a bed. Nothing about the sheets or the whiteware tries to impress. If the owners ever decided to sell the workers lodge, nothing inside would be sold. Everything would be given to charity so that the goodwill box could be ticked, where it would likely gather dust before heading for the dump a few years later.

When I entered, I was pleased to see one of the other kitchen hands, Joey, kneeling over a pile of scrunched up newspaper and kindling in the fireplace with a lit match. I'm pretty sure Joey was always stoned. There wasn't a lot of variation in his reactions. He had the same cackle for everything, no matter the degree of actual hilarity. 'Liam,' he greeted me with a nod, as he always did. I made my way to my usual room – two bunk beds, except my usual bottom left was frustratingly already occupied by another – their territory marked by sheets they'd clearly brought from home, a phone charger plugged in, the cord hanging lazily, and a pair of ski gloves left near the pillow.


There's very little to do in Drift other than work, eat, drink, or head up the mountain. There's none of the usual town suspects – no library, swimming pool, community centre, or school. On my days off, I usually slept in. Then, eventually, once I'd run out of sleep to be had, I'd rug up and wander down to the shops. For lunch I would have either a bowl of fries and a burger from Dusty's, or a footlong Subway. I liked to eat outside if I got Subway, standing on the corner of Glen and Elk. I'd stand and watch or stand and be watched while lettuce shreds fell out the bottom and landed in the slush. Most of the time someone would wander up to me, a worker I knew from the chalet or the mountain or the bars, and tell me I was a brave eater. Other times strangers would trudge past and tell me I ought to think about going inside, didn't I know it was -19°C? But there was something about the habit I took great pride in, and there wasn't a lot I took pride in. I was freezing and I was eating outside when I could be eating inside, a fool's choice.

I'd arrived with one day and one night to spare before my shifts started up, and so I dumped my bags in the bottom right bunk, where Toad used to sleep before Camille from France arrived the first season he didn't show for and took his place. Camille had tattoos from Bali and gemstone necklaces and came back three years in a row before eventually amassing enough money for a year-long meditation retreat. Then came Alex from Seattle – he didn't talk much but boy did he snore. Now it was me. I didn't bother making the bed and headed out for a Sub.

It was later that night, at Dusty's, that I first met Gabriel. There were six different televisions showing all kinds of extreme sports – snowboarders falling down vertical mountains, skiers gliding enormous zigzags just shy of snowed-in craters, alpine climbers at Everest-equivalent altitudes. Everyone at the bar was either getting drunk because they didn't know anyone or getting drunk because they knew everyone. Gabriel seemed to be the former. He was sitting at the bar studying one of the televisions when I walked in. I intended to ignore him and head over to a group of more familiar faces, but he struck up a conversation while I was waiting to order my drink. He was handsome in that kind of innocent way, a bit pretty, almost too much so, with long eyelashes. He was clearly intelligent, well-kept, but timid about it all. I let him keep asking me questions and I asked some myself. I forgot about the friends I'd wanted to favour and slipped onto the stool next to him. We took turns buying rounds and his speech and smile eventually got looser. He told me he was from Vancouver Island, that he went to art school, that he struggled with the desire to make art but also the realisation that art could only offer so much, and with some negative comments about his own talent, talked about how he'd recently decided it was time he applied himself to something more practical, like nursing, or teaching. Drift was his first season. He wanted to make some extra money before going back to school. He'd grown up outdoors. He wasn't usually a big drinker.

I'm still not sure why I spent so much time with Gabriel at the bar that night. He was conventionally attractive, but I wasn't that attracted to him. I only said hello to my old friends once or twice on my way to and from the bathroom. Something about him needing me was appealing – the way he looked at me gave me permission to think highly of myself. When I took him to the bathroom, it felt like I was taking his virginity. I liked the way his small bottom hung in the air, waiting for me, when I unbuckled his pants from behind. His hair was curly and smelt freshly washed. He dressed in clothes that neither intrigued nor bored me – I can't remember exactly what he wore, only that he had blue woollen socks on beneath his boots, and that when I came, he got up on his tippy-toes. Afterwards, he said 'Thank you' with flushed cheeks and I told him not to worry and immediately rebuckled my own pants. I let him give me a kiss before we left the cubicle and returned to the bar.

I wasn't so keen on sitting together just the two of us anymore and so I brought him over to my regular friends and introduced him, let him be swallowed by the introductions, then went out to smoke a cigarette, watching as the exhaled smoke ballooned in the freezing air as if my mouth were a volcano erupting. Then, I Irish-goodbyed and walked home. It wasn't until later that night, when Gabriel stumbled into the bedroom, that I realised he was the one who had occupied the bottom left bunk bed. 'Goodnight,' he said into the darkness, and I almost said it back, before deciding to pretend I was asleep, and turned my attention to Joey snoring from the bed above.

The next morning, I felt all kinds of things. One, I did not enjoy waking up. I was hungover and our room smelt of booze and, dare I say it, I missed the smell of Xavier's and my life – expensive musky perfumes and scented candles. I half expected to wake up to someone cracking a joke, as was the usual, but then I remembered who I was rooming with. My stomach felt light and heavy at the same time. Joey leant over the bars of his bunk to yank the stiff curtain back and white light poured in. 'Jesus,' he mumbled, then burped. I went to the kitchen and made myself a coffee. Thought about what I was feeling. Was I pissed off? Not quite. Was I tired? Not only. Too hungover? Perhaps. Feeling guilty? Maybe. I considered whether there was such a thing as a diminishing return in Drift. Was there a cap on its promise to you? Or was I just being sensitive? Or was I just not settled in yet? Or was I getting old, and this is what hangovers started doing to you? I sipped my coffee. I had a hot shower. I left.

My first shift went by fine. We were employed by the lodge, so we only encountered people either about to head up the mountain or about to spend their days waiting for their family members to return from the mountain. I was with Frankie and Joey and neither of them had anything funny to say. Frankie told me about her latest relationship and Joey told me about his investment plan in a local paragliding company. We carved the ham. We scooped the roast potatoes. We poured the gravy. Lodgers came by with their plates, staring at the brightly lit trays, sometimes looking up to smile, sometimes chatting away to one another – questions of which peak to head to that day, will they take their Quest or PowderPro gloves? Et cetera, et cetera. Once upon a time, it had been Toad who got everyone giggling. He was bouncy and jokes just zinged out of him like extra energy he needed to release – otherwise he might have just compounded. I'm not sure where his neuroticism came from. During shifts, once the drunk feeling from the hangover wore off and things dipped out of the silly and into the cumbersome, he'd fish out whatever small bottle of spirit he had on him and pour it into cans of Coke. Then everything became hilarious again. He'd look at me with big wide eyes and giggle manically. I felt tame compared to him. Which made me feel good. I felt like a loose end when I was with Xavier. With Toad, he became me and I became Xavier. But Toad wasn't me, he was Toad. And Toad was life. One particularly boring shift, Toad handed me a baggie. 'Just a little bit,' he said. Just a little bit was also what we did as soon as the shift was over, and at the top of the ski field, and in the cubicle at Dusty's that evening, and right after we had sex. God, Toad and I could fuck. He was a skinny guy, but he had a beautiful penis – long and wide enough to make me gasp like a little girl.

By the end of the shift, I was ready for a ski and a drink. Frankie went home to shower and Joey and I fished beers out from the kitchen fridge. Joey's a nice guy, but he's not one to contribute. He'll never tell a story or suggest an activity, but he is a yes-man. If Frankie had said, 'Hey, Joey, it's time to shower,' he would've. But I got there first with my, 'Hey, Joey, it's time to go up.' He was my back-up friend. Company when that's all you needed. When we reached the entrance to the slopes, we were already five deep. It looked the same as it always did. Automatic doors swinging open and closed as people wobbled in with their boots, like astronauts touching down on the moon. Melted slush on the linoleum floor. Queues of people lining up for the bathroom before joining the queues of people lining up for the chairlift. Posters with bright block letters advertising whatever parties would be taking place in the bar that week. I looked at Joey, expecting him to look back at me so we could exchange a knowing smile, but he just kept walking.

In the line for the lift, we came across Gabriel. He was with Frankie, exchanging polite musings on the politics of extended families. Frankie spotted us first, punched me in the arm, then Joey. We were all dressed up, goggles and all, so I could only make out a faint smile from Gabriel, and it was difficult to know whether it touched his eyes. I felt that same unease I'd felt in the morning. It annoyed me. I guess I was annoyed I'd slept with Gabriel. I'd told myself I wasn't going to do that kind of thing anymore. It was a promise I'd made to myself and broken enough times that even I knew it was getting ridiculous. We shuffled forward. It was clear two groups of two had become one group of four by the way everyone was standing and facing one another, which only annoyed me more.

By the time we reached the front of the line, the chair lift picking Gabriel and Frankie up, then Joey and I, I'd decided it was fine. It was fine because what had happened with Gabriel was a one-off. It was fine because it was a mistake. People make mistakes. The important part is not letting it ruin your life. I let it go. I held the bars of the lift excitedly. Looked down at the skis hanging off our feet. Passed a small bottle of tequila to Joey and chugged my own.

---

Nobody cares how much you drink up the mountain, just so long as you don't pass out. The best part was, no one thought you'd fallen over cause you'd drunk too much, just that you'd fallen. There was no order to what we consumed. Frankie and Joey knew that this was how it was, but Gabriel seemed surprised when we reached the peak and didn't immediately head for the slope, but for the bar instead. 'I'm pretty hungover from last night,' he said, and Frankie just laughed and handed him her flask. I watched as he winced, but I didn't feel pity for him, if I'm telling the truth. I knew I should have, I know I should have, especially now. But I am trying to be honest about who I was, and what I felt. And in that moment, all I could think was how there was something so feeble about him, as if he were a baby bird that needed stronger wings before he could learn how to fly.

Xavier is different in this way. He would never drink shots and the last time he was up a ski mountain was probably during a school trip. The only regular exercise Xavier does is hiking, which he plans and prepares for more than is necessary. When he's on one, I always get a text stating his location and start time, and another when he's returned safely. As if hiking for three hours off a State Highway is particularly dangerous. But what I do respect about Xavier is his fondness for using the word 'no'. It grates me, sure, but it gives me something to butt up against. Let's get one more drink after the movie? No, he has an early start. Let's get some cocaine? No, it made me feel strange that time five six seven eight nine months ago we did it. Let's buy this really expensive bottle of champagne? No, it's not budgeted, and we need a new couch more than we need alcohol. Frustrating, but it gave me the confines within which to live, and the confines in which to break in Drift.

Gabriel, on the other hand, seemed to only have the confines other people had given him, and no clue whether he wanted to break them, or even who had given them to him. He was one of those people, I imagined, whose sense of identity was often in flux, in a more dramatic sense than most. I tested this theory by ordering another round of shots. Could Gabriel become Toad, if the expectation was laid on him? When he shuddered, tucking the lemon slice into his lips and wincing, I laughed. 'You gotta act like it's the best thing in the world and then it will be,' I said. Gabriel took the slice out of his mouth and laid it on the bar. He smiled and nodded his head shyly towards the door leading outside. Not quite a Toad clap-your-hands-together and yell *yeehoo!* before bolting for the snow – but it was something.

⁂

Together, the four of us made our way down the mountain. I purposefully skied behind Gabriel so I could watch his movements, how he moved from left to right, inspecting him for signs of inebriety. It was hard to tell. You could always tell with Toad, but then again maybe you couldn't. He'd lift off from the snow on his turns, if he had the speed, then switch the other way. Sometimes he'd straight-line it, gathering so much speed that he'd become a speck in the distance, then you'd turn a corner, and bang, there he was, holding out a bottle of whatever. It was difficult to know whether he was brilliant or stupid, or both. Gabriel seemed to be being careful, slowing down whenever he started going too fast. I supposed I was halfway between them. I never flung myself about like Toad, but I liked to go fast. When I went fast, I could feel everything and nothing at the same time. The calculations in my head ticked away at speeds they never could back home. My body moved like a machine. Left to right. My mind made sure I was never in danger while my body pushed itself to the limit. Right to left. It was always a moment. Left to right. Never did I finish a run and think it wasn't worth it.

▲

I missed Drift whenever I was back in Vancouver. It's outdoorsy and it has nightlife but the two have a well-mannered crossover. It's walking or kayaking with cocktails and small plates. Whenever I was sitting on our couch, typing the words someone else was speaking, staring out the window at the river, I often returned to thoughts of the mountain and the madness of it all. How, when the day was done, your energy would somehow not be fully spent, that, if anything, it was maximised, compared to the exhaustion I felt from hours of typing, and we'd be headed straight for Dusty's. Whenever I was leaving Drift, back on the bus, I'd tell myself I was going to find a way to bring that vitality back with me. I'd go paragliding, get a new job that got me out of the house, try new food, start swimming nude, get Xavier's and my sex life back up and running with some kind of activity-based game. But when I returned, normal life always managed to make its way back in. I did go paragliding, one summer, and Xavier came to watch, and once I'd landed, the whole rush from the experience was minimised by a single 'that looked awesome' followed by a pat on the back.

🙡

A month went by, and Gabriel was peacefully indoctrinated into our way of doing things. It began with the petering off of his complaints of a hangover, then he began purchasing his own stash of spirits, and pretty soon, just as expected, he was taking his turn as instigator so that the role never sat with anyone long enough for them to second guess themselves. It was a carefully unspoken rota. 'Dusty's?' he'd say after the last run, or, 'Beer?' when we entered the bar doors, and, eventually, 'Coke?' or, 'Molly?' or, 'Ketamine?' I'll admit I enjoyed noticing his eyes on me, or these suggestions being directed at me. There were, regrettably, a handful of occasions where I found myself back in the cubicle with him. Which, if I'm being honest, which I am really trying to be, only ever happened after he hadn't shown me much attention, and was talking to someone else, or not within a certain radius of where I was, and I felt the power he normally gave me beginning to slip away. Power is fragile and insufferable. It's scary being honest, and even now, I find myself trying to tell only parts of this story, to impress, or to reason with, whomever I find myself speaking to. But in truth (ha!) I am only speaking to myself right now. And is there anything more difficult than being honest with yourself? Because, well, I'm acting like all of this is special, but it happens every year. I find someone, or someone finds me, and I regret it, and I do it again, and then I let it go, and they either get sick of it or they get sick with love, and then it all goes bottoms up. Toad, then Harry (a rebound from Toad), a few kisses with guys I don't remember the names of, and Anthony who used to work the bar at Dusty's. Rob, an Australian who wore baseball caps and still messages me sometimes. He'd been the last. It had been a clean year till Gabriel came along. It had been clean because every year was clean until I returned to Drift. I'd thought this time would be different; I was getting old – but clearly not old enough.

▲

About a month before the end of the season, I saw Gabriel on the street near the bus depot. Behind him, fresh tourists were unloading themselves, parents deboarding the buses were calling their children's names, and the bus driver was hauling suitcases and backpacks onto the snowy footpath. He hadn't seen me, and I watched him for a while, how he scuffed his shoes into the snow, and slowly moved his mouth, chewing on a piece of gum. He too seemed to benefit from Drift. Where I had seen a timid, well-kept city boy that first night at Dusty's, I now saw a tanned snow boy. Someone who could drink and smoke and build a fire and would never, ever complain about a hangover. Behind him, the doors of the bus closed and the last of the tourists disappeared, and then the bus drove away, revealing an elderly woman standing at a white table with red flyers and a donation box for some form of charity. She tried to wave me over, but I wandered over to Gabriel instead. 'Hey,' I said. I asked him how he was and listened to him tell me about his day, how it had started off well, but after a stressful work shift, had gone downhill. His voice sounded sad. It also sounded to me like the kind of thing that just happens in life. But I said the right thing, which in its own way, was dishonest of me. I asked Gabriel what had happened and offered the sort of suggestions everyone would offer him. Kindness and honesty do not bode well together in my world. Gabriel's eyes began to water. I took him in my arms and rubbed circles around his back, like I did with Xavier when he'd tipped from tense to distraught.

'Drink?' Gabriel said when we uncurled ourselves from the hug. His eyelashes were wet and stuck together. I nodded. The woman at the white table with the flyers tried to get my attention with another wave but I turned away before my eyes could make contact with hers.

We sat in the booth near the front window of Dusty's and drank beer. 'Don't know if I was just being naive,' Gabriel said. 'But I'd thought being here might give me a bit of a break from getting stressed.'

'Difficult to get away from,' I offered. I had to keep my replies as generic as possible, I realise now, in order to avoid talking about myself. Now, I'm not one of those people who can't talk about themselves. I just think there's a certain amount of value you can get from talking about it a certain amount of times.

I think a part of the reason I love Xavier is that everything that a relationship requires you to know about the other has already been cleared. We know what has hurt the other and what still hurts. We know what not to talk about. We know what to make light of. Know how the other likes to live. I love how boring he can be. Life, for him, is set in place. Sectioned off and lived to the fullest within firm lines. One large supermarket shop every Sunday and a top-up shop on Wednesdays. He was not always boring. It came out of necessity, I believe, in order for him to avoid feeling like his life was unravelling, or that he was going crazy. Being raw to the world can also mean you're ready to be beaten down. And some can manage that better than others – for Xavier, misunderstandings with friends got him so blue he would need to stay in bed for two days. And the same went for work, a stranger on the bus, the checkout lady at the local grocers, anyone and everyone. So, through trial and error, concrete methods were put in place. No late nights, no holidays with friends longer than three days, regular wake-up times. No screen time past 7:00pm, one hour of reading before 9:00pm. I loved Drift for the way it allowed me to appreciate what Xavier and I have in Vancouver. I loved Drift for making me feel like I liked the way I lived. It's not that I ever actually wanted to live in Drift. It was unsustainable. But in the same stroke, living in Vancouver was unsustainable, in all its organised glory.

'It is nice to let loose though,' Gabriel said, in agreement with my internal monologue. 'I feel like I'm always trying to fix things, but here, I can let go.' We took large sips in unified agreement. He continued. 'I don't know when I started being an adult, but it feels like I've been living life by a list that never ends for so long. You go to university, you get a job. Pay your taxes, spring clean, recycle, catch public transport, invest in new furniture, lose faith in takeaways, only drink on dates. Question your current job, restart the whole process.'

'Only drink on dates?' I asked.

'Well, yeah. I get too tired at work otherwise. But dates, well, I've been trying to make more of an effort to put myself out there.'

'Admirable.'

'Hardly,' he smiled. 'My track record isn't exactly great.'

'Maybe if you drank more on the dates and cared less about the work, you'd have more success,' I said.

Gabriel laughed a little. 'That's what you do, isn't it? Encourage people to drink?'

I felt taken aback but quickly laughed. 'You should've seen the guy who got me into drinking.'

'So you're the trainee. And I'm the trainee's trainee?' he smiled.

It was the first time I acknowledged Gabriel had his own understanding of what was going on. That he had, along the way, been perceiving me, judging me, as I had been doing to him. I recall looking into Gabriel's eyes and feeling oddly seen. Like we were on even standings. I was no longer not crazy enough (for Toad) and not organised enough (for Xavier). A meeting of the malleable minds. We spent the rest of the evening jokingly exchanging digs at one another, occasionally dipping into periods of psychoanalysis (of his exes, family members, and himself), until we were both so drunk we started forgetting our sentences midway through saying them, and descended into fits of laughter instead.

When we got home, the lodge was empty. Remnants of a fire and a scattering of empty cans provided evidence of an earlier social gathering that hadn't included us and had since moved elsewhere. Gabriel boiled the kettle and I sidled up behind him, wrapped my arms around his waist and let a stray hand make its way slowly, slowly, to his crotch. I massaged a soft bundle of penis until it began to take shape, felt Gabriel's head slowly roll back until it was leaning against my shoulder. I kissed his neck slowly while I unzipped his pants, turned him around, and got on my knees.

⁂

A few days later, we awoke to Frankie coming into our room. 'Excursion,' she announced. 'Next weekend.' She drew the curtains back. The sun still hadn't risen. 'Did you know it'll be our last free weekend before the end of the season?' Across from me, Gabriel readjusted his pillow so he could comfortably sit up.

'No way,' he replied.

'No way to the excursion or to the end of the season?'

'End of the season. Where're we going?'

'Tambre, about a half hour away. The slopes are closed to the public for a worker's day. There'll be, like, sixty people max across all the routes. And they're having a party. DJ Marx is playing.'

'Who?' I said.

'Doesn't matter, get excited,' she said, clapped her hands, and left.

For the rest of the week, talk of the excursion resurfaced again and again. It was like it was New Year's Eve, the way everyone had so easily pinned their expectations to it. As if everything everyone had hoped would happen over the course of the season would be given permission to happen in Tambre. Unactioned hook-ups, unconsumed drugs, failed ski moves. Apparently, Tambre was going to allow us to out-fuck, out-party and out-perform ourselves. The energy rubbed off on me. I found myself in trances, pulling drumsticks from chicken carcasses, ladling gravy and peas and mashed potato onto people's plates, fixated by blurred images of snowy ice caps and twenty-dollar notes rolled into tubes, travelling across white lines.

Like most things you get excited for, when the day of the excursion arrived, a franticness had attached itself to the anticipation. The lodge was filled with half-packed bags, buses home or buses to the airport only a day or two away, and thoughts of what would come next had begun to take hold. Gabriel spent a lot of the shuttle ride to Tambre on his phone, tapping out long messages. I avoided my own phone, vaguely aware that it would contain a message from Xavier, detailing the pick-up time and the evening we would spend together upon my return. Somebody played drum and bass through the van's sound system, a bottle of tequila was passed around, and beers were downed. Yet no matter how much I drank, none of it seemed to be enough. I was sad, I realised, looking out the window as tall spindly trees coated in snow were left behind and rapidly replaced by others.

I was still sad at the top of the mountain. The rest of the party was at the bar, listening to the first DJ set as the fun began to ramp up. In moments like this, the upward route to drunken climax, I normally found myself in the centre, or at least, on the outskirts. I'm still not sure why, instead, I went to the chair lift by myself. At the top of the mountain, I clicked my skis off and sat in the snow. In front of me, the sky was blue. Red flags marked the edges of each runway, and, beyond the mountain, a vast expanse of white and dark green stretched out ahead of me. It was beautiful, and I hated it. But I also loved it. I didn't understand how I could hate and love so many things and people at the same time when others seemed so capable of sorting them to one side or the other. All the thoughts in my head had false starts, and unable to give any of them the proper time of day, I took more swigs from my flask and stood to reclip myself to my skis. I surveyed the empty slopes beneath me, and tipped my skis so that gravity could take me, and began my descent. The alcohol had definitely made its effect known, despite my own assertion I may as well have been sober, because the only thing I remember is a fast journey that still managed to feel slow, and sluggishly falling over multiple times. I recall feeling the same emotions I'd had at the top – alone, and not just in the lonely way – in the haunting way too, like I could sense the weight of other people around me. A cutout of Toad on my back, and Xavier, ahead of me, moving horizontally through the snow with gentle ease.

⚘

When I returned to the party, I found Joey leaning against the bar with his goggles lifted to his forehead and an ungloved hand flicking through a dating app on his phone. The walls of the bar were almost entirely glass, and everybody was milling around the DJ booth. Clusters of brightly coloured skiers trudged towards the lift outside. I still felt on edge, and ordered a drink and sipped at it while offering light-hearted commentary on whoever Joey paused to look at long enough. It eased me back into the party mode. Soon, Joey and I were relocating to a table and playing Shoot, Shag, Marry with celebrities and countries and drugs and the people around us. Marrying Spain and shagging France and killing England was enough to counterbalance whatever thoughts kept trying to make their way to Xavier, to Toad, to Gabriel. Looking back now, I think I was sad because I was afraid of the burgeoning possibility I liked Gabriel after all. It was not that I was head over heels for him. I was just surprised by how it felt. Like we were two young boys who didn't know we were gay yet. Like I was coming out for the first time, all over again.

When Joey stood and told me he was heading up the mountain for a run, I was pleased to find Gabriel swiftly taking his position in the seat next to me. He looked tired, and drunk. His eyes were wet and there was a small amount of white attached to a clump of his nose hairs.

'You having fun?' he said.

'How could I not?' I raised my beer to the room. It was a sight for sore eyes. Snow had been walked inside and had since melted into puddles on the rubber-backed mats. Gear had been stripped off and dumped into large rainbow piles. Everyone working the bar looked miserable to have to put up with everyone. The DJ looked as if he expected a larger crowd, and the crowd looked like they'd been stubborn about the exclusivity of the event and now regretted not inviting more people. It was still too light outside for anyone to be hooking up, but it was clear groundwork flirting was underway in how people were standing and talking in twos.

'It all feels a bit frantic,' Gabriel said.

'That's 'cause it is,' I laughed. 'Welcome to the end of the season, where everybody recalibrates themselves for their return to the real world by consuming copious amounts of alcohol and drugs.'

'I can tell that's the goal,' replied Gabriel. 'But I don't see how it's meant to help.'

'Think of it like a reset,' I said, and took a long sip of beer. 'You get so fucked up, that the next day the hangover is so awful you actually want to go home.'

Gabriel raised his eyebrows and nodded. 'That actually kind of makes sense.' He took a long sip of beer too. That same sad look came across his eyes.

I patted him on the back. 'It's time to go up,' I said.

He smiled. It felt good to make him smile. We got two drinks each for the ride. We went to the bathroom and did lines off the top of the toilet dispenser. We got back into all our ski gear, drunkenly giggling and helping each other zip various zips.

The chair lift scooped us up and we began our ascent. I could spy Frankie ahead of us with two others, and clouds had rolled in so that the peak was no longer visible. I was relieved to find my lonely excursion now felt like a faraway memory. Below us was the sound of skis and snowboards carving lines along the tracks. Gabriel and I drank our beers and tried to point various people out. It was difficult to know who was who unless they had a particularly trademarked item, like Joey's bright yellow beanie with an upside down smiley face printed on its front. We blew hot breath on the exposed hands holding the beer. We giggled at one another. For a moment, just a moment, it felt as if Gabriel and I were our own kind of couple. And it was sweet in a way that the other people I'd hooked up with had not provided. There was an innocence in how he operated, an innocence I was surprised to discover I still had.

'What's the first thing you'll do when you get back to Vancouver?' he said.

I shrugged. I'd never mentioned Xavier to him. 'Not sure,' I said. 'Probably get dinner.'

'Where from?'

I thought about this for a moment. We would, most realistically, go to the local Italian restaurant. If I were with Gabriel, I considered, I'd suggest Chinese takeaways at home. We'd do something cosy, like watch a film or play a board game. It would be cute. Gabriel was sort of like a teddy bear. Xavier was an expensive breed of bull. Toad was some kind of antelope on speed.

'Pearl City is good,' I replied. 'Down the road from mine.'

We'd reached the top. I lifted the bar, and we slid off, skiing to the side. We made hand signals to one another about which route to go down. They were all difficult, but different kinds of difficult. One run was almost completely vertical at the beginning, and so you had to spend the first few minutes doing horizontal lines and harsh turns that often dropped you down a few metres. Then it eased out and you looped your way down the mountain. The other was gentle at the beginning and became increasingly steep, eventually culminating in an even longer stretch of vertical that I often found myself on my back for. But once done, it also eased itself into a nice glide.

Gabriel didn't seem to care, the way he was swinging his hand in the direction of both runs. I watched as Frankie toppled on her side on the vertical-start, giggling, and nudged my head towards the other. I preferred to put off the falling over until some fun had been had.

We began. God, I was drunk. I let Gabriel ski ahead of me. For someone just as drunk, he held his own pretty good. I no longer had Toad on my back or Xavier ahead, taunting me. Instead, I think I felt some kind of peace. There was a light tethering between Gabriel and I that was neither frantic nor suffocating. I know it's possible it could have been escapism pinning itself to a different narrative. But in that moment, I was so drunk I thought I loved him.

We paused about halfway down and sat on the edge of the halfpipe. A couple of people bolted down, and paused to stop just ahead of us to puke. I couldn't tell who they were, but they waved and laughed in our direction. Gabriel gagged a little and hocked some spit into the snow. I ambled over to him clumsily, lifted his ski mask to his forehead, and kissed him slowly.

'I come to Vancouver sometimes,' he said when we pulled away. 'You know, to see friends. I could let you know next time I'm there.'

I nodded and started kissing him again. It got more heated. If it weren't for the snow and the people zinging by, I would have had sex with him right there and then. Instead, we kissed until our erections were busting and we had to stop. We laughed and restrapped our gloves.

'You ready?' I asked.

'Ready as I'll ever be.'

We began slowly – moving from left to right and back again. For a while, we didn't let ourselves catch any speed, as if we were waiting for the other to say something, but as time went on, and we both remained silent, we let ourselves glide a little less and bolt a lot more. It's strange how quickly it happens. One moment, you're like a kid on a seesaw traversing down the mountain, and things are lively yet calm. Then, if you let yourself, you're going so fast you're in a tunnel with walls of sky and snow that change at speeds your mind has no chance of truly seeing, only processing. Gabriel was still ahead of me, with his knees bent, poles lifted off from the snow, and his zigzag had almost completely become a straight line. He was zooming. I followed suit. We passed the two people who had been vomiting before. The bar where the party was still going came into vision as a small speck and someone in a chair lift above screamed 'yeeeeehoooooo' at us as we bolted past. My heart was racing. My vision was hazy. I'll admit I became scared. There was the small notion of feeling like I wasn't so invincible after all, and I thought about slowing down, even just a small amount, and yelling after Gabriel to do the same, but it seemed ridiculous. I kept going. We kept going. A corner came up, and I let myself drag my left ski so that I eased into the curve a little slower. It still wasn't enough – I lost my grip on the turn and completely bowled. My skis pinged off in opposite directions and I felt my right ankle twist with it. We were, I realised as I began to slide, on the edge of the vertical slope. On my back, I stuck my elbows into the snow as I fell ten, fifteen metres in slow motion. My head hit a bump, but I kept sliding. Halfway down, I was able to stop myself completely with my elbows wedged into the snow, pinioning me to where I was. I looked around me, but everything was blurry. I lay there. I wondered whether the minutes would become a few hours. I'm not sure how much time did pass, but what felt like soon after, Joey was standing above me with my skis under his arms, jokingly reprimanding me for choosing the gnarliest route when I had almost certainly been the one to drink the most that day. He clicked his own skis off and helped me into mine. My ankle was shot and my head felt fuzzy.

'Mate, you're bleeding.'

I touched my forehead. He was right. 'Did you see Gabriel on your way down?' I asked.

'Nope.'

'He was ahead of me, before I fell.'

'Must have left without you' he chuckled. 'Want me to call a sled?'

'Na,' I replied. 'I'll go slow.' We went carefully. It felt like my head was full of fluff. Near the bottom of the vertical, Joey pointed off to his left. 'Is that...?' he said, looking towards where the slope dropped off to a scrabble of rocks. It was heavily marked with a row of bright orange fencing, and it was common knowledge to hang right as you descended this section. A tourist had died there three or four years ago. There were signs at the top of the vertical that warned you against it. Next to one of the orange fences was a single ski, as if someone had tried to click their skis off to brake and stop themselves from going over and had only managed one and not the other. Joey and I went as close as we dared before taking off our own. We lay on our stomachs and dragged ourselves to the edge. My vision was terrible. But I could still see, metres down, face down in the rocks, the body that belonged to Gabriel. It looked as if he were sleeping the most uncomfortable sleep. I could only look once. Joey started screaming out his name. 'No,' I yelled. 'No, no, no.' Tears began to stream down my face. Joey got out his cell phone and called for help. I couldn't do anything. I kept yelling out the word 'no' as if someone had asked me a question.

I don't remember much else from that day. A helicopter came and flew Gabriel out, and not long after, a ski patrol sled came and strapped me in. I don't know if it was the alcohol, or a concussion, or just pure shock, but I remember the events that unfolded afterwards like still frames, and I can only click between them as if using a slide viewer. Two-dimensional, without sound or smell. First, there is the square of sky above me as the sled descended – pale and meek. Then there are the trees outside the window of the ambulance that came for me. Third, a hospital bed with empty seats at its foot. Then again, only this time with Xavier in one of them, quietly reading a book. I am told I spent four days in and out of consciousness due to internal bleeding in my skull. It is apparently a miracle I'd been able to get up after my fall, and incredibly stupid of me to try and keep going. When I was eventually able to start thinking and talking for myself, what had happened on the mountain felt like a strange and hazy dream. 'Gabriel?' was the first thing I asked. I'm not sure if I was asking where he was, or whether he was okay, but I think I already knew. 'I'm so sorry,' was all Xavier could say. He never has been good at telling people what they don't want to hear.

After law enforcement officials came to take witness statements, I chose to only look out the window of the hospital room. I watched as the snow melted and the season came to its inevitable end. The trees outside were thawing. Days flitted by, and Xavier dutifully came and went from his hotel room, bringing with him food and magazines with sudoku puzzles. Occasionally, he would try to make conversation, but mostly he just left me alone.

After about a week, the nurse discharged me, and Xavier and I drove back to Vancouver. 'Do you want to talk about it?' he asked, turning onto the State Highway that would lead us back. The car smelt so clean. There was a pottle of chewing gum in the cup holder. Xavier's hair, despite being away for over a week, looked the same it always had. 'Not really,' I replied.

'That's understandable,' he nodded.

We barely spoke after that. Xavier kept the radio on a low volume the rest of the way home.

Gabriel's funeral was arranged for the week after we returned, on Vancouver Island. Despite still being cold out, his family insisted on having the entirety of the service outside, on the seafront. To get there I had to drive along roads that wound through a forest filled with trees not unlike the ones found in Drift, only these ones had already started sprouting new leaves. I parked my car among over a hundred others next to a lodge I later learned Gabriel's family used to holiday in before his parents divorced. It was overcast and windy, and there was the constant cry of gulls overhead. Young deaths always amass a crowd, but I was surprised to see just how many people had known Gabriel. We gathered where the trees thinned and stood facing towards the ocean, where a pastor stood on the shoreline and spoke through a handheld microphone. Speeches went into the late afternoon. Friends and family members told stories of Gabriel being cheeky and loving. Teachers spoke of Gabriel's intelligence and generosity. His mother wept about how sensitive he had been as a little boy, how open-minded about the world he had been as a young man, how much she had loved getting to know each new part of him he revealed as he grew older. A lot of people described him as shy until comfortable and referenced his bad dance moves. I stood next to Joey and Frankie on the left-hand side, behind what I can only assume were Gabriel's real group of friends. As the service progressed, they took turns holding each other, laughing or crying at certain stories.

Afterwards, Joey, Frankie and I went down to the water's edge and skipped stones. Everybody was slowly making their way to the lodge where there were drinks and nibbles, and a book for people to write down their memories of Gabriel. The three of us exchanged some quiet comments on how we were still in disbelief. I watched, out of the corner of my eye, as Gabriel's mother walked around the people still outside, and told each of them there was food if they would like some. When she eventually came to us, she asked how we'd known Gabriel. Frankie explained we were new friends from the ski field, and she searched Joey's and my faces for signs of the boy who had been with Gabriel before his death. I smiled at her sadly. My injury was covered by my hair, but I sensed she knew. I thought about admitting it was me, but then she looked away, and started speaking. 'Gabriel loved it here,' she said. 'I'm still not sure why he wanted to go up a mountain when he loved the sea so much.'

⁂

We mingled at the reception for an hour or so. We three felt like intruders, like strangers, and so we stuck together in the corner, exchanging odd remarks on how it must have been nice to grow up on Vancouver Island. Frankie was the first to announce she better be going, and so we walked outside with her and said goodbye. Joey and I shared a cigarette on the lodge steps. I felt ill, sitting there, listening to the chatter coming from inside, all evidential of the love Gabriel had had in his life. When I got back into my car, I checked my phone and saw a text from Xavier asking what time I'd be home. Instead of turning off to get back on the highway, I kept going along the coastal road until I reached a dinky sort of motel on the oceanfront with shutter doors. An old man in overalls gave me a key to one of the back rooms. It was small with windows that looked back towards the forest. I changed out of my funeral clothes and thought about whether to go back outside, back to where I could see the ocean. Instead, I got a beer out from the mini fridge, sat on the edge of the bed, and listened to the trees outside shivering in the wind.

🌲

And it is here that I recount this all. I'm not sure how long I've been sitting here, maybe an hour. It is the most profound sense of sadness. So sad, that it transcends into no emotion at all. I had thought that by combing through these events, I might be able to make some sense of it all, or come across some detail that fixes things, or realise a turning point, a moment where I made this happen. But it is a series of them, and it has changed nothing. I keep looking out the window as though the outside world is going to present me with a choice and my reaction will split my future in two, then again, so there are four, and again, to eight, and again, forever ad infinitum. The question, I realise, is what to do with this event. The two choices I imagine would be the most distinct – a world where, overcome by guilt, shock, and the rest of it, I live with my regret long enough to put effort into righting my wrongdoings. Sit in parks and think about what I've done kind of thing. Break up with Xavier, give him a chance to live his life without me kind of thing. Apologise to Toad kind of thing. Never go back to Drift kind of thing. Work in nursing or teaching for Gabriel kind of thing.

The second route forwards – a world where I keep going, as per usual. Remove the evidence in front of me. Recalibrate it with versions of stories that allow what I've done to sit in my memory as a silly time marked by an incredibly horrible event. The clouds outside have begun to close in, and the forest in front of me has become dark. I let the two world routes peel off from one another like fuzzy yellow balls on a tennis court. It's like they're soaring slowly through the air, out there, as though stuck in thick fog, coming up and over the spruce trees, towards my decision-making racket. Behind me, I can hear the sounds of a mop bucket pedalling down the hallway. I turn to see who it is, but my bedroom door is closed. When I turn back to the window, it's too late. The ball with redemptive qualities is soaring for my face, and it's terrifying, terrifying to have to face all that guilt, so terrifying that, if you will believe me, it is actually impossible. Survivors' instinct is a real and flawed thing. To take on redemption would be to call my whole being into question. I hit it clean out of the court, and off it goes, out over the trees, and I catch the one of ignorance firmly with the free hand of my mind. For a moment, I pause, as if it's still possible to swap them out.

Which it is. The other balls are still out there, all ad infinitum of them, soaring from other hands, other places, and though I might have caught this ball, who's to say something couldn't knock it out of my grip? Who's to say I won't wake up tomorrow and change my mind? I listen as the tree leaves continue to rustle in the wind. It's already beginning – the start of the new season, and the new narrative, the one where I had no say in Gabriel's fall. One where my treatment of him had nothing to do with the cosmic misfortune of his death. One where my trips to Drift were ones of refuge, not of debauchery. One where the world is fucked so you may as well just make sure you have a good time. No way to make it better (never!). The only way to make it better is to think you can make it better. I thought once more about what to do, as though second, third, fourth guessing myself might make the guilt of the first decision a little lighter. Which it does, in its own strange way, because then it feels like more time is spent on letting it go.

# BAD KID

Carol, all warm and giddy in her chest, dipped her big toe into the little pond and exclaimed to the kids, 'The water is so tepid! The water is so tepid!' Wanted them to do the same, take their tiny sneakers off, the ones the big brands made so cute with their miniature logos, and dip in their pigletty toes. Hoped it would bring about some magic in their lives. Imagined them as parents themselves, telling their own children about days spent in the garden with their Ma, doing silly little things like toe dipping or having sleepovers in the treehouse, or even that time they played Survivor when it rained. Carol swirled her big toe through the water some more. Heard deeper versions of their voices saying, 'O, and how it rained! But we wouldn't eat, refused to! So Ma, well she boiled up eggs and hid them around the rose bushes so that we could pretend we were living off the land.' HA. What a joy their family was and always would be!

But the children did not seem to get it. Ruby just said, 'Ma, what is teh-pud?' and Finn shoved her and replied, 'Not teh-pud, teh-*pid*.'

They really did not know when to pick up a good time that was coming for them. But this was how children learned, Carol reasoned, lifting her foot out of the pond and gesturing for them to come closer.

If Steve was here, he would think, *Wow, what a spontaneous and loving mother. Look at my family, outside, kids breathing in fresh air, no TV, learning how to have a good time with one's imagination.* That was something Carol's mother never did for her... no. It was all clean that and clean this and no elbows on the table and listen to your father or you're disrespectful, my God you're so disrespectful!!!

'Yellow car!' Finn yelled, and punched Ruby hard in the arm.

'Owwww, there's no yellow car,' she moaned.

Carol could not help thinking, *Wow, that moan is annoying; hope she grows out of that.* Then she turned to Finn, shook her head, and said, 'That is no way to treat your sister, apologise,' which he did.

Did kids not know how to untie one's shoes? Sheesh. They were still just standing there, Ruby rubbing her arm, tears not quite breaking free from the lid, and Finn looking up at the sky as an aeroplane passed over. Had always been obsessed with planes, ever since he was a wee thing. Carol thought, as she often did, *I wonder if he'll become a pilot? Or will his passion for cutting up food and plants overtake? And become a surgeon, or a biologist?* Ruby, Carol wasn't so sure yet. A teacher, perhaps. Good thing was, they could make up their own minds when the time came. For now, their minds just needed to bloom. Carol bent down and began untying their laces.

Now that their little toes were out, the three of them stood on the smooth stones at the edge of the pond while Carol showed them how to toe-dip. No full footing because of the goldfish, Lollipop and Band-Aid. Kid's ideas, and you bet, Ruby wanted a lollipop at the time and Finn had scraped his knee. Still, Carol loved to tell people her kids had come up with the names. How silly they were! Such silly, free-spirited, children!

And what a silly, free-spirited family! Steve, bless him, had spent the night before all sore from playing hide and seek with the kids after work. Then when she, Carol, was giving him a foot rub while they watched their TV show, the kids had burst back into the living room, even though it was well past their bedtime, squealing, 'We found you! We found you!' and instead of going all, 'You should be in bed, grrrr,' Steve grinned and said, 'You found me, you found me. How'd you do it?' and they'd all laughed, big roaring laughs, and the kids had come over for one last cuddle, and she, Carol, had given Steve's sore feet a squeeze and a smile that said, I'll handle them, you rest, and he'd smiled back a smile that said, God, I love you and I am oh-so grateful for you.

So, she'd woken up that morning, all loved up on her family and thought, *to heck, why don't me and Steve go on a date? When was the last time we went on one of those?* Sure, they weren't always great. There was always something, but they always worked it out. Not to mention his face, when she'd said it, had positively lit up.

Hence quality time with children before the babysitter arrived. New babysitter approximately twenty minutes away, old one doesn't work so well for last-minute romantic dates of people who have been together fifteen-plus years and still love one another. Not to worry, Carol is organised – always ripping those tags off the babysitting posters at the school!

⚜

Maia, sitting on the edge of her bed, checked her phone one more time before leaving. Yep, definitely expected at 6:00pm. And yep, address definitely only a fifteen-minute walk away. Stood to look in the mirror one more time. Had recently discovered that body equals appearance – had not always thought that way. Was only twelve after all. Before this revelation, body equals for running, playing, jumping. Now Maia had those things called boobs, but more like pre-boobs, not like other people's real-ass-chunky-boobs. Chunky? Not quite right. Round, shapely, full. Nice to look at. Had recently also discovered magazines, and flicked through them whenever she did the supermarket shop. Maia was convinced that one day, soon, she would wake up and see that her celebrity body had taken over. Not today, though. Maia ran a hand down the curve of her belly, picked her backpack up off the floor, and walked outside.

Front door slammed shut behind her.

'Honey,' her dad said.

They were both on the porch, him and Nanna, all sombre like. Not that what they were doing – sitting in their armchairs, looking out at the street, waving as people passed by – was sombre, just that when Maia stood near them, she smelt it felt it. Bad vibes. Cigarette smoke and half asleep.

Maia knew people thought their family was strange. Sometimes, kids and mothers stopped to point at the windows of the house, where they could see items piling up inside. If they stopped, Nanna would start telling them stories and they'd pull happily on excuses of needing to get somewhere or check on something. On Halloween, children with mothers hurried past while unsupervised kids could be heard running into the property, yelping, 'I'm in the haunted house! I'm in the haunted house!' while others shot back, 'You're only in the front yard!' followed by squeals as one of them would run closer, then pull back and return to the safety of the road.

Maia loved her dad and Nanna, though. Really loved them. Reckoned she would love them even more if she had her celebrity body and they spent their time cleaning instead of on the porch. But no, loved them anyway. Loved them extra. That was how love worked. Would always love them, would always care. Hence babysitting. Little extra cash for a little extra nice times together.

Waved hello and goodbye to them. On her way she went, along the street, keeping to herself. Could hear her thighs touch themselves, swish swish. Thigh gap. Maia learned about this one not in magazines, but on the internet. The internet is still pretty new, not that new, but new enough that it's very slow and their computer is very large. A little like her bottom. Just last week, when they were eating sausages and bread for dinner, Dad said, 'Maia, careful, too much white bread will make your bum too big!'

Maia figured her butt and thighs were to blame for lack of thigh gap. She felt her face getting warm as she focussed on the way each thigh squished against the other with every step. Decided to move thoughts elsewhere. Cool how she could do that, Maia and her brain. Like, wonder what this woman's house is gonna be like, being all on the nice side of the suburb, the side that neighbours a rich suburb not a poor one.

Thoughts moved back – not so cool how the brain did that. Began to think about Lily, Lily being Maia's best friend, and how she still had a body like Maia's. Lily's family a bit odd too, Maia thinks. Too many kids for two parents to have (nine!). Maia didn't tell Lily about magazines or internet discoveries, though. No, something told Maia this stuff was private – there being a reason why computers and magazines were for one person to use at a time.

Behind the front door was the sound of a yapping pup.

Carol opened the door. The hallway rug lifted slightly with it. 'Welcome! Come on in!' she said with a cheery voice. Always felt a sense of pride bringing people into her home, all clean and lovely, but not sterile. A family home. Patted the rug down with her foot.

Nice feet, Maia thought (little white fluffy thing still yapping). Seriously, how did her feet look so soft? So pale and smooth? With the hard skin all rubbed off? And polish without chips? None of those red lines made from tearing at the skin? Wow!

'I'll show you around,' Carol beamed.

Kitchen first. All shiny and no food in sight, Maia was like Wow! – again. Even the bread bin matched the appliances. Nothing like their kitchen at home, which felt grimy, even when they had done the dishes.

Carol bent over the dishwasher, hair falling all silky over her shoulders. 'We normally run it once during the day and once at night, but I forgot.' Then she bent back up again. 'You look familiar,' she said slowly, then paused. 'Who're your parents?'

'It's all good,' Maia gulped. 'Deb,' she said. 'My Mum's Deb, we live a few suburbs over.'

'Oh, I thought you—' Carol began. 'Never mind.' She turned to the fridge and pulled out a packaged dinner. 'The kids love this one, so you shouldn't have too hard a time getting them to eat.'

Nothing like this in the world, Maia thought, sitting down after the kids had gone to bed. What. A. Couch. So damn comfy, soooooo soft. And who'd have thought packet chicken pie could be so fancy? Organic seemed the word. O-r-g-a-n-i-c.

Mmm-mmm, maybe the house was organic too? The wood and the couch and the vases and Carol's hair and Carol's toes. Well, Wow! Better soak up more of the house, Maia thought, and stood up. Wandered into Carol's bedroom and the guest room. Found mirrors in both, and lifted her top to inspect what was beneath, in case any changes had happened, which they hadn't. Opened the drawers of each bedside table. Watches, sleeping masks, vitamins, ear plugs. Ran her bare foot along each rug. Found secret heaters, camouflaged. Every pillow had a pillow. So! Much! Stuff! But organised in that way where you don't even see it? Hidden closets, hidden cabinets. Compared to Maia's... sheesh. Back to the kitchen. Maia opened up the pantry, stepped inside.

Face to face with cereal, nuts, muesli bars. Chocolate flavoured with things like plum and pear. Nuts and cereal all got a green o-r-g-a-n-i-c flag. Ate a lil of most things, just a lil. On the top shelf were supplies for baking. Baking anything. Birthday candles for every kind of birthday, cupcake cups with ribbons, toy trains, Christmas trees, stars, ghosts, and most shades of the rainbow. Maia walked to the living room, sucking on a square of chocolate. What the hell kind of computer is THAT! Tapped its spacebar until the screen flickered to life. It didn't look anything like the computers at school. Clean and white with an apple printed on its front. Maia guided the mouse to a button with a rocket, and a game popped up. Eh, Maia thought, and closed the window. Clicked another, with red curtains? Then, Maia's face appeared in front of Maia's face, all spooked looking. She leaned in closer, still spooked looking. Willed Carol's face to appear instead of her own. Or at least her celebrity face. How come her hair doesn't do the silky thing? Or blonde thing? Why did her eyebrows look like little rabbits, about to scurry off her face? Maia leaned back, body looking like the top of an ice cream cone, or a cupcake, sheesh. Leaned back in, clicked the button.

3-2-1. *Boop*. Blur of mush.

Maia clicked the button again.

3-2-1. *Boop*. Shiet! So mush.

Well, research, Maia thought.

Got to know what one looks like to know where one's going.

Maia took her top off.

3-2-1. *Boop*. Bra just looking like a bra on an ice cream cone!

3-2-1. *Boop*. What the heckers. No better.

Took many more research 3-2-1 *Boops* of all angles – front, back, left, right. Even took her bra off and retook all angles, realising her boobs would likely be a key part of upcoming bodily transformation.

Sat back down and sighed her way through the photos. Where was her bikini body? Maia dragged them into the trash bin. She knew enough about computers to know one must always dispose of questionable items. Walked back over to the kitchen counter, where the leftover chicken pie sat. Cut another slice and ate it standing up. Cut one more, then settled back into the couch, saddened. At least, Maia reasoned, she was a good daughter. She'd buy one of those chicken pies next time she did the shop. Never had seen them at their store though, and had bought many frozen pies during her lifetime?

🜲

God, kids are running Carol up the wall today. Life is running Carol up the wall, if she is being honest. Why could life not just stay in one place? One happy lovely place? Finn refusing to wear sneakers to school, not cool enough. Ruby, refusing to eat oatmeal. Wants Cocoa Pops. All sugar!

Steve out of the house before the kids even got up. Stressed with work. Poor Steve.

What would fix this? What would her mother do and

how would she, Carol, not do that? Mother would yell – Carol is going to stay calm. Put a little sugar on Ruby's oatmeal, tell her it tastes better than Cocoa Pops. Get Finn to play his game he loves and put shoes on him while he's distracted.

Ah, coffee. Everything going to plan.

'Mum, what's this?' Finn goes, sounding all grown up. So proud of him, sounding so adult for his age, Carol thinks.

Please, oh God, no, God. No, no need to swear in her head. Just remain calm, in... out, in... out.

'Finn, that's enough screen time for now,' she says, and shoos him off the chair. 'Go and brush your teeth, you too, Ruby.'

And they do, God Bless them. They know when to leave Mummy alone.

Carol clicks through the images. At first quickly, then very slowly.

Remembers discovering filthy magazines under Steve's side of the bed when they first got together. Felt so sick, so sick. Forgave him, eventually, without ever speaking to him. Took great courage to do such a thing, to allow one's partner to have urges not involving she, Carol, and let it go. Continue building their family, their home.

A sexual little girl in their home!

Spends the whole morning deliberating, fretting. Considers calling the police, but no, that's what her mother would have done. Carol would do the sensible thing. She would send the girl a message:

## BAD KID

*Hi. Saw those pictures you left in the trash bin. I hope you didn't send them to anyone, because those are not the types of pictures one should be sending. We won't need you to babysit again, and please stay away from my children.*

Stern, but not harsh, Carol thinks, and clicks send.

🌲

Mrs. Adaway is saying something about assembly being cancelled when Maia's phone buzzes. Can't check it just yet. Is too busy listening to what Jessie from the second row is saying about the school dance. 'You can't wear long skirts,' is what Jessie's whispering. 'And mullet skirts are even more out. Mini-mini's are in.'

Maia gulps. Thighs still only getting wider. Just that morning, Lily said she was going on a diet. 'Diet?' Maia asked. 'Thought those were for old people!'

'For us now, too,' Lily replied.

*Gawd*, Maia thought. One good thing about life was food. Not to mention the school dance only a week away. Maia checks her phone. A message from Carol!

Sick, oh god so sick. Sick in the stomach, sick in the heart, sick in the toes.

Whole body light then whole body heavy. Something in her throat.

So sick that Maia can't cry. So sick that Maia can't think to go bathroom, just sits there, in her seat, not looking at anyone.

'Oi, you okay?' Lily says at lunchtime. 'You look sick.'

Maia can't do anything but nod. Spends the rest of the school day with her heart in her throat and cheeks.

On her walk home, Maia finally cries. Feels like a creep, like a danger to children. Walks the long way home so as not to pass by the primary school. Remembers when she was a child, running around the playground, with no idea about anything.

Wonders whether Carol has told anyone, like Dad.

Sick, oh God, so sick again.

What if Dad's told Nanna?

What if granddaughter being a creep tips Nanna over edge into death? Move thoughts elsewhere, move thoughts elsewhere, move thoughts elsewhere!!!

Begins to cry, panic cry.

Through the gate, at the front door.

↟

Carol goes outside. Dips her toes into the pond – alone this time.

# IT WAITS

I couldn't quite believe the summer that had laid itself out for me. A sweet, slippery mat that couldn't manage to hold onto a single person, feeling, or event. Totally fictional, we all were. We'd done what we'd always done – spent the winter months popping days into a piggy bank that looked at us with painted eyes and promised us everything would be okay again once things were warm. As though we too could be placed in an oven and rise into a loaf of something lovely.

But as the warmer days had edged closer, disruptions began to ping around the walls of our lives. First, my girlfriend – the one I had imagined a life with, the first one I had ever imagined a life with – announced she was moving to London and was not interested in a long-distance relationship, and a gut-wrenching separation ensued. I loved her, and still do, as frightening as that is. Then, Timmy's German uncle was revealed to be a paedophile, a particularly bad one at that. Not long after, my cousin was hit by a car on his way to buy drugs and was killed instantly. Elia, my best friend from high school days, arrived back from her home in New York and announced she was no longer in love with her boyfriend of eight years. All around us, life was dying or falling over.

*Hot girl summer*, Elia messaged as I laid out in the first sunny day trying to singe my skin. *Nice person summer*, Timmy corrected her. I wasn't sure what it was to be nice anymore. Did it require a giving away of kind words, or an item? But was it still nice if I said those words in an effort to be nice? (*it can be a hot and nice person summer*), or if I didn't want the item anymore, and it aided me to get rid of anything that reminded me of her? So, I decided to be nice was to simply not disrupt, which meant to sort of float, to not exist.

The first thing we decided to do – Timmy, Elia and I – was to get jobs somewhere that would allow us to swim and drink as much as possible. So we moved to Bayside, located on the precipice of eternal summers, where even in winter you could find leathery sun agents applying sheens of coconut oil to themselves.

There were a lot of smells that hung in the air in Bayside – the clean factory plastic of activewear, hot corn chips from everyone's favourite chain restaurant, and the dull zest of acai berries obliterated into smoothie bowls. There was also the stench from pottles of party food left to harden overnight, and the tinny smells wafting up from the piles of cans slumped against the corners of everyone's front yards, with juicy blowflies making their rounds.

I think the town was designed that way – to home everything that made you feel on top of it, whatever *it* was – jamming you with organic promises and exercise-fuelled pleasure chemicals, so that you never had to admit you were on a never-ending cycle of waking up to rid your hangover in time to accrue another.

🟊

Another pull was that our friends – Jules, Linda, Jacob and Luca – JLJL I liked to call them in my head, for they'd been moving as a pack for as long as I'd known them, and quite honestly, I wasn't sure what they were like on their own – had a shared house we could join them in. They had jobs cleaning the beaches that were technically meant to be volunteer roles, only the organisation was low on sign-ups and had received donations to pay temps, which we also tagged ourselves to. People were always coming and going from Bayside – some living, some visiting, and even the ones who set up shop there swanned about in a permanent state of vacationing. So everyone, even the not-for-profits, was desperate for the half-assed employees we were.

We began our days the way we ended them – in bed, lulled but not lulled enough – nothing was ever enough, until an aspiration was stirred up somewhere within us. A desire to be tired, to have something to fill our days with, to add a few dollars to our wallets, and we were moving through the sand dunes stabbing colourful rubbish with pick up sticks as though we were hungry for a healthier environment.

'I wonder whether Albie knows I don't love him anymore,' Elia said one day, and we put our rubbish bags down on the dunes and surrounded her in kind words, trying to scrub away the guilt so clearly twisted up inside of her. We'd been avoiding pain together our whole lives. It was when Timmy told Elia that love was a gift you didn't always need to be giving that the boss, in her branded conservation coat that read SAVE OUR BEACHES came over to me with a clipboard, moved her pen down a list of names, and told me I wasn't meeting my pick-up quota. And it was when she said this that Elia raised her eyebrows high enough that I knew she thought it was a joke, which it was, it all was – life was! But it was when I realised this that someone sprinting over the white sand came into vision with a hand up as though miming a telephone. I turned my focus to a deflated purple packet of Doritos woven into the sand, but the steps came louder, and louder, until the man was in front of us, yelling that he needed a phone, did anyone have one, please call an ambulance, someone had broken their hip and was stuck in the shallows. He was lanky but with some muscle and a head of hair that looked like it had been bathed in salt water his whole life. I thought maybe I could sleep with him, that maybe his penis might not be as tan as the rest of him, but it could be an advantageous way of getting over the ex-girlfriend, to have sex with something that she would never be able to give me, but then I realised I don't like penises, only the plastic kind strapped to a thrumming vagina, and that this man still needed a telephone. I fumbled in my pocket and tried to hand it over.

'No,' he said. 'I need you to call the ambulance, he's over there, I'm going to get someone strong enough to help drag him out,' and off he ran towards the more muscular volunteers.

I stumbled down the dunes away from the group, acutely aware of them watching me as each step pushed the granules of sand further down the slope, a slide of steps until I reached the compounded flat of the shoreline and began to sprint over to where the wet-suited man was spluttering on his side, waves rolling him around while he cried out in pain. I tried to lift him but was too weak. I looked back at my phone, realised I still hadn't called emergency services, and began frantically hitting the necessary buttons. Soon enough the tan man was back with another man, and they were lifting the injured man out of the waves' reach, all the while grunting and gasping from either exertion or pain. I stood there, listening to the operator tell me how far away the ambulance was, and began to draft the entire experience, as it happened, into a story I would tell the others later.

※

Later, later, later that evening we washed the salt from our hair and put a song on that signalled the tossing of bottle caps and the pulling back of can tabs. Soon, everything felt okay again. Then it didn't – Elia said something about Timmy's German uncle's sentencing – until we drank ourselves back into ignorant bliss again. I waited for JLJL to come home before I told the story of the man with the dislocated hip – how I'd ended up having to wait on the road in my bikini until the sirens came into earshot and I could begin waving them down. How the man had started to giggle when the ketamine was injected, and then the man with the tan had presented me with a beer and I wondered whether enough gifts from him could make me straight again.

'If only things were that easy,' said Elia, and asked whether I had the hots for any women we'd encountered.

I'll admit sometimes I thought about all of us getting it on, Timmy, Elia, JLJL, and I, but not in the erotic way I'd want to fulfil. It was more that we were all a part of something – a shared way of living, that it felt only natural that we would create even more symbiosis by orgasming in a room together.

'I think the boss might be gay,' I said instead, 'but I'm not sure I'd go there.'

⁂

Two gulls on the end of the wharf, fucking, the carcasses of shucked seashells splayed out around them, was a little like the first time the beach boss and I had sex. Hot and smelly in the way you don't know whether you'd rather put your whole body in a bath full of ice – pain and fingers in you, slap me on the ass, put your fingers in my mouth, I might come! Oh, I might come! I need to leave, you all of a sudden smell like a paper bag that's been holding meat, or – nothing but pain? I chose both, and spent my walk home searching for something, anything, to tell me that I was real. I selected a flag, waving outside the surf rental shop, displaying two kiwis surfing a comically cryptic wave of colonial New Zealand memorabilia, which transported me back to the flag referendum, to the design the Prime Minister promoted that resembled the branding of his political party, and then to the design of another kiwi wearing sunglasses that shot laser beams somewhere past the flag's material remit, and right into me, laser beams shooting through my heart as I walked along the pavement, and someone in the park was playing techno music, and I was receiving each note as a pixel in my stomach, and no one could stop me, I was walking home to have a drink.

A few days later, Timmy bought himself a bunny. He thought about calling it his child. 'Child, come here,' he tried it out. Then he decided it sounded mildly paedophilic, and tried a rolodex of other names – Kath, Kim, Turtle, Torpedo, T-rex, Jennifer, until arriving on Callum. A white fluffy thing with red eyes started to hop around our house, everyone chirping and cooing *ohhhh Callum* whenever he managed to do something that made his psychotic blood-bathed eyes look a little cute. A changed man, that's what we said about Timmy. He used to drink-drive and get into fist fights, but with Callum, he became a parent. A parent that, when faced with small pebbles of rabbit poo in his bed, decided it was fairer to put his own bed in a cage so that Callum could have free reign of the rest of the bedroom – high jumping over the metal cage every night and falling asleep to the sound of Callum's mouth muttering. Timmy even brought the bunny on our outings, and we joked that no bunny had ever experienced such a varied life.

One afternoon, we drove over an hour to a nearby river – Elia and I up front, Timmy and Callum in the back seats, JLJL in another car trailing behind. On the edge of the water, Callum sat patiently in Timmy's lap. Elia stood in the shallows of the river, unmoving, like the smooth river stones beneath her feet had birthed her and she'd grown, year by year, in that very spot. I looked at the bushes she was stuck staring at and saw her boyfriend Albie's face, morphing between hurt and anger, their house of five years peeking out from each branch, leaf, tree. I went underwater, became a fish, then a seal, a ray, an eel, armless, legless, genitalless, hopeless. I wondered whether staying under would force me to grow gills. Above water, Timmy cracked a beer, Elia awoke, moved her head to him, and asked for one too. I did not develop gills, gave up on the body of water holding me, and rose out of its depths. Dripping across what was dry before, towel under me, can in grip, sip sip. JLJL had told me, at a party the night prior, that it appeared the ex-girlfriend was already seeing someone else. At the time, I had broken down. Then I chose to feel nothing.

Nothing was also how I felt later that night, back in the arms of the conservation boss. We had, through a series of awkward glimpses on the job, graduated from disgusting seagulls to shy sparrows, unsure of where to put our feet or how to chirp, and going nowhere near the thought of fornication.

'I'd like to take you on a walk,' she said, peering at me sideways from our spot on the boardwalk bench.

In front of us, waves crashed in the darkness. The only light came from the streetlamp above, encircling us in an orange glow that made me wonder whether we could be something more than sparrows or seagulls. Two eagles, ambitious, or two dolphins, silly for one another.

'What kind of walk?'

'A long one.'

I took a sip from my can. 'Will we take whiskey? Whiskey is good for walks,' I said, returning to a memory of a four day hike I took with JLJL and two other friends around a lake, where we underestimated how much food we'd need in favour of overestimating the volumes of whiskey. Still, we finished it all, taking dribbles from the nearly drained bottle, drunk and a little sick from the swaying bridge we'd sat on and the absence of dinner.

'I like to do my hikes sober,' she said, and I wanted her to be a seagull again.

🌲

It rained on the day she chose – thick hot drops that made the bush feel like a rainforest. She asked a lot of questions – and we rose. I gave her everything in clipped answers – my high school origin story, the biographies of family members, friends, exes, the ex-girlfriend, some stories of Elia and Timmy, until we were above the clouds. The tip was singular, becoming small from each direction until a flat circle about two metres wide was presented to us. Too even to be a mountain top, I thought. So she kissed me and I hadn't a clue what kind of bird we were, so high up.

⁂

One night, we hosted a party, in which Elia insisted we each write down something we wanted to get rid of to throw in the fire later. Standing at the time, Elia passed me a shred of paper, and I took a brief step inside myself, considering what to write. Then a song changed. A glass slipped through Timmy's hand in the kitchen and broke into chunky pieces. I stuffed the piece of paper into my back pocket, listened to the shout of somebody asking where the hell the rest of the party was. To pass the time, we took turns going into a confessional booth that was actually just the bathroom, already puddled in footsteps, to privately declare to a recording phone who we thought would get the most drunk. I elected Timmy – and just an hour later he was keeping one eye shut to stop everything from getting together.

Not long after that, the house was full of barefooted boys in ripped singlets and surfers with boxes of beers tucked under their arms. The women, who shared names like Rach and Jess and Beth, sat themselves in an organised grid. Completely unfuckable, I thought, then felt bad, and reached for the piece of paper in my pocket, which was a sort of prayer. Index finger and thumb rubbing it soft, *please stop me from looking at the world the way I do now*. Too difficult to put into one word, so I'd simply tried out the word PERSPECTIVE, then scribbled it out and tried OUTLOOK, as in my entire way of viewing the world. The prayer didn't do much – the girls still looked like strange pretend extras, so I took a gulp of wine, two, three, then asked if they'd been given a piece of paper yet.

'For what?' the one with the gelled back ponytail asked.

'To write down something you want to get rid of.'

I set a piece down in front of her, continuing along the row like a teacher handing out worksheets. I imagined her writing down something like *my bum* and was taken aback when I saw her loopy swirls spell out the word *overthinking*, quickly folding it up before anyone at seated level could see.

At around 9:00pm, Elia emerged from her bedroom, hair redistributed in only the way profusive making out can do, a terribly guilty look on her face, and so I guided her over to where JLJL were sitting on their knees around a coffee table to play drinking games, as though we needed the encouragement.

Meanwhile, in Timmy's room, just metres away from us, planks of wood snapped beneath the pressure of a boy called Aaron lobbing his body – twenty-three percent of which was comprised of alcohol, eleven percent of his thoughts directed at the term *root* as in fuck as in sex – onto the bed. Other keywords and associated synonyms included *piss, kiss, Kanye,* and *manu*, the reo term for the bomb technique Aaron had used, where arms are used to hold knees and the human body hurls itself ass-first, typically into water, but in this case, onto Timmy's bed in the exact position needed to crack the base and land upon Callum the bunny, who was hiding from the noise of the party, snapping his neck not quite enough that he died instantly, but rather experienced at least one minute of pain, eventually drowning in his own blood – the same colour as his eyes

– bubbling up his throat. It was another six minutes before Timmy decided it would be hilarious to assess the damage done to the bed base and hoisted the mattress up. Glass cracking in his throat, his cries swallowed the entire house and its occupants whole. From my position on the couch, I briefly entertained the thought that someone had just vomited on him, but no one was laughing.

After a few sentences of contorted support for Timmy, we participated in a silent game of selecting who we'd like to spend our time with post-bunny-death, retreating to various rooms with our counterparts to wait out a decision on the appropriate thing to do. Elia and I spent our first ten minutes together in a regrettable kind of way – avoiding Timmy – laughing and crying before Elia told a neighbour over the fence that 'our friend's bunny just died.'

Then, we shut up and drank till our heads were balloons and we took the strings and led them into a bedroom not already occupied. Elia lowered her hand into her bag like a claw machine, coming up lucky with a bag of ketamine and eight pressed pills in the shape of Bart Simpson's face. I thought about the man on the beach with the cracked back, cracked wood, cracked bunny head, and wondered how he was doing. Strange I hadn't thought about him till then, white powder nipped into my nostril. By the time we left the bedroom, a cacophony of doors opening, people emerging from their drug dens loose in the body, still tense in the mind, the party had transformed into a funeral reception minus the funeral or the reception.

Timmy, crying, alone, had carried the bunny outside, wrapped in pyjama pants and placed in a dresser drawer.

Somebody whispered a story about a child that loved his bunny so much he squeezed it to death.

On Timmy's signal, re-entering the home with a false grin on his face, we all pretended nothing terrible had ever happened. The ketamine had taken effect and so we clomped our legs around the house, slowly neighing for everybody to move to the garage where somebody had set up a dance floor. I went to the bathroom, stood in front of the mirror, assessing what was in front of me and imagining the various places I could put my body. In the arms of her, in the arms of him, but which her, and which him? Her or him, him or her, her or her, him or no one, no one or her.

Two bodies flunked onto the wooden hallway, and I caught my face as a stranger in the mirror. Outside, the boys had taken it upon themselves to mop their own spew up with dishwashing detergent, proceeding to use the slippery passage as a slide without a slope, instead using the front yard as a run up.

'Is it safe to come out?' I yelled, and they replied in laughs.

I cracked the door ajar and saw them on the floor, legs knotted together, their shirts dotted in wet patches, abandoned pieces of paper with words like *jealousy* and *ego* and *aggression* soggily plastered to the floor.

Elia's head popped around the corner. 'This party is dying out,' she said, and I imagined us all being able to slip the night into an envelope, lick it closed, and discard it into a post box.

'Who wants a go?' one of the boys yelled, and I forgot the image of the envelope and instead wondered whether his stubble would scratch me if we kissed. Then I thought about the ex-girlfriend and her mouth on a highway of other mouths, kissing and kissing until all of our own kisses were but a distant memory in the backlog of other kisses, and then an image of her standing on my doorstep one day, explaining it away until it didn't make my heart hurt, only sing, but then the song hurt because it was a song I was imagining, and very rarely does something you imagine actually happen. You think the thought and the thought flies away from you and so you think another thought. If such a thing were to ever happen, a reconciliation of sorts, it would feel nothing like how I'd imagined it. It would be sitting upon whatever years of thoughts I'd had until that moment, on that day, that day that might never happen. No point in worrying about it now, and so I tapped a message out to the boss: *are you out?* and put it into my back pocket, walked past the bunny cemetery, and entered the garage.

Flicks of ginger fur rose up from the concrete road. Attached to it, a kitten's head, the criss-crossed pattern of a tyre pressed firmly into its crown. Our car swayed to the right, out of the kitten's way. The night before did not know what to do with us. When you're that hungover, nothing can stick. Body becomes play dough, brain cream, the world around you putty in someone else's hands but they're offering you the puppeteering rods for a laugh. We had just finished eating our first meal of the day, but we were somewhere else. Brain was with the kitten, smooshed into the concrete, heart was with the bunny, buried, lungs were with the fireplace, ashed out. What was left, with us, was pickled. The flesh on our bones had fermented, and all we could think to do was buy another box of beers. We drove to the beach, sat in a row like we were waiting for the ocean to teach us something, taking sips when we felt it was right.

'Did you sleep with someone last night?' JLJL asked Elia, taking a swig.

'No, but I made out with Aaron, the bunny murderer,' she whispered.

The sky above us shifted tact. No longer sunny, but a little silver.

'What about you, miss fuck-the-boss?' Elia asked.

I laughed, took a sip of beer, and felt the waves laughing back at me.

I offered them a version of the story that was much more entertaining than the experience had been, and drained the last of my bottle, pointing in the direction of the box as an ask for another. Elia passed one over, flicking the cap off with her lighter.

The text had gone the way someone who sends that kind of text would hope – though I still wasn't sure what part of me the words I'd written belonged to. The lonely organ or the clitoris, the survival segment of my brain or the ego. The tricky part of not knowing where a desire comes from is not knowing whether it's been met. An absence of measurement, an absence of fulfilment.

We had, after spending another few hours at our separate parties, congregated in a drunken stumble on the boardwalk, coming together in an embrace and a kiss that felt more akin to a battle than anything affectionate. For the row of us that sat on the beach, I phrased this part as, 'We met up and made out on the boardwalk,' and they all giggled before sipping again.

After we'd unlocked mouths, she'd brought out a packet of cigarettes from her bag and told me she didn't usually smoke, but that she'd had a big night. She sounded a little like the ex-girlfriend when she'd said it, and we sat in silence afterwards, passing a cigarette back and forth. I looked at her in her earnest brown eyes and thought about the ex-girlfriend's eyes, all sparkly and green and unemotional.

She started to talk about work and her aspirations for the beach, how she'd met a man that wanted to donate just under a hundred thousand dollars, and wouldn't it be great if the group could expand, and move throughout the regions, removing tinsel from the shores?

I took a half-drunk bottle of wine out of my bag and took swigs until I felt aroused and began to ask questions about her sexual history. The best sex, the worst sex, the most surprising sex. She regaled a story about her own ex and the sustainably built luxury treehouse they'd spent three days in, only ever taking a one or two hour break from fucking. Then, something about a sweaty boy in a public bathroom that I chose not to tune into, happily lingering on the first story. For this part, I simply told Elia, Timmy and JLJL that we'd sat drinking and smoking and sharing sex stories. In its simplicity, it was steamy. In actuality, I remember feeling disturbingly fascinated with the idea that I was an oil rig, and each question let me mentally dip into her, trying on her experiences in my imagination so that I no longer had to use my own. By the time we got home, drugs fading away, morning shining in, bunny in my head, I'd felt too weak for sex. I was too tired to tell my fellow ocean-watchers this. Instead, I stood up, and they stood with me. Elia, Timmy, JLJL and I. We began to walk forwards. At the dry line, we took our clothes off and went to the waves like we were falling, chanting wishes in our heads of something else.

⁂

It turned out it was not exclusive to the bunny, or the kitten's head. It was a whole thing. Everything kept dropping quicker than flies – two women in the shark alley, one child in the park, and a pod of beached whales – even the man with the broken hip, I learnt during a run-in with the man with the penis, had only a forty percent chance of living due to the severe blood clots surrounding his fracture. It seemed today no longer mattered. What was important was that it left and joined the yesterdays, that even if people and animals and plants were dying, very soon they would just be a part of everything that had ever died. But the one death we could not shake, for whatever strange reason, no matter how many drinks were drunk, was that of the bunny.

'Everybody asks Timmy how he's going without Callum, but no one ever asks how I'm going,' a voice from within JLJL said one day.

We all blinked, including JLJL.

'My sister died, only eight months ago,' the voice said.

I stuck my fingers into the files of my brain and was able to retrieve only the outline of a memory.

'Oh, that's right,' Elia replied. 'Man, that sucks.'

⁂

That night, moving our feet in circles across the linoleum floor of the liquor store, I swore I could see my face in it, it was so reflective, we decided to buy JLJL the best tequila our money could buy. Then we argued in front of the mixers fridge about whether to buy ginger beer (which Timmy had vomited up too much of) or orange juice (which reminded Elia too much of being hungover), and whether we should purchase additional beers or wine, and decided to buy it all as a celebration of our being sympathetic to JLJL.

Back at the house, Timmy decided it was about time we did a jigsaw puzzle. We had four of them, a 1,000-piece depiction of the leaning tower of Pisa, two New Zealand wildlife scenes, each 500 pieces, and something called the Raconteur, which was part of a so-called Piece Full puzzle series designed for mindfulness. They had come from the same miraculous land that all jigsaw puzzles came from – no owner, just arriving on any slightly odd ledge beneath a table that needs something on it.

'I can't believe we're doing this,' Elia laughed, and lowered herself onto the floor, turning pieces of the puzzle right side up so that we could begin to separate chunks of sky from chunks of the tower from chunks of the grass. The tequila appeared, then disappeared, then the wine, then the mixed drinks. We were playing the merry soundtrack of our lives, opening vessels and sipping from them like they were our instruments, singing our favourite line – 'I can't believe we're drinking again.'

'This is nice,' Timmy said.

'This is nice,' Elia replied.

We sipped some more, slowly moving through the pile of cardboard pieces, clicking the corners into place.

'This is nice,' Timmy repeated, locking three pieces into a corner.

'This is nice,' JLJL chorused.

'This is nice,' I heard myself saying, and then Timmy said it again, and then we were all saying it, until I wasn't sure who was saying it. We all were. A peculiar combination of affirmation and persuasion. It dropped to a whisper, *this is nice this is nice this is nice*, moving piece into piece, interlocking them, building the picture until I felt we were a puzzle of our own, taking and giving from one another, whole together, a bit useless alone, JLJLTE and me.

Then, just as involuntarily, Timmy stood up. 'This is not nice,' he said.

'This is not nice,' JLJL confirmed.

Then Elia was saying it too, and I was looking at her with a bruised heart, and she was looking at me the same, and they were all saying it – this is not nice this is not nice – while they walked away in different directions, and it became a horrible dance, watching them from my kneeled position on the floor while they separated. J became Jacob, standing on the deck and lighting a cigarette, looking forlorn.

'My sister died and all you think to do is buy more alcohol,' he said with tears in his throat, before dragging the door closed behind him. Then, Linda began sobbing and went to the bathroom. Jules went to the kitchen and began bashing plates around. Luca walked down the hallway and we heard the front door slam behind him. Elia was still seated next to me, turning a puzzle piece over in her hands. 'This is not nice,' she repeated, and bent over to begin slowly packing the puzzle up, which wasn't even a quarter complete.

I couldn't bring myself to say it back, and remained sitting there on the floor as though I had it in me, which I did, but it never arrived.

'We're going to be okay,' I said, and she smiled back at me in a sad sort of way.

'Tomorrow, we'll figure it out.'

⁂

That night, all of us under one roof, sleeping like pandas that had too much to drink and fucked up a jigsaw puzzle by getting upset, I felt lucky. I remember feeling something strange when I thought it, a kind of tinny taste on my tongue that reminded me not of drinking beer from a can but of being children and laying our tongues on any surface we so desired. Mud, rust, car, tree bark, gravel. It was so quiet I thought I could hear all their singular breaths, until it became one whole breath, and the house itself felt like it was alive and dreaming. I'm not sure when I fell asleep, but it was sudden and it was deep, and I dreamt a very ordinary and practical dream. In it, I was picking up a staffy dog from the pound and giving it a name and a collar. Then, I was taking it home to a house I lived in alone. It was filled with things I did not own yet. A little messy. I was not particularly sad or happy in the dream, and I even recall acknowledging this in my sleep. I cooked some porridge and lit a fire. To light the fire, I had to go outside and chop up wood. The dog nestled into my lap,

## IT WAITS

and I sat there, a little calm, a cup of tea in my hands, of all things. I even wrote a grocery list that became a series of jokes. That is all I remember, but it was the first normal dream I'd had that summer.

⁂

In the morning, I woke to an empty house. I yelled out their names – and when nothing came back, I stood at the neighbour's fence and yelled some more, but still no response. I went into their bedrooms, one by one, and discovered everyone's furniture but mine was gone. A faint outline of the blood stain was still etched into Timmy's carpet, but it was more faded than before, as though someone had spent the whole night scrubbing it. I thought there would be a note somewhere, and so I went to the fridge, but it was blank. Same with the front door. When I opened it, I half-expected them to jump out from around a corner, *boo!* and throw a water balloon in my face so I could scold them for being silly and get on with the day. But still, only quiet. I ran onto the street, where I thought they might be hosting a garage sale, or had perhaps piled all of our belongings into a moving truck that we would be keeping in storage until the next summer – but quickly realised the street was empty, and my room was still full. The air was still, too. There were no cicadas kicking their legs or neighbours mowing their lawns or kids skating along the pavement. I was alone, and so I began to walk, and I realised the whole town was alone – a great overnight excavation had taken place. There were no cars in the driveways or on the road, and the shops were all closed. I tried to peek through their shutters, only to discover the window displays were empty and all the lights were switched off. Even the liquor store, which normally had boxes of alcohol piling up at the entranceway, was desolate. Along the main road, the billboards had been stripped of their advertisements. The cinema was boarded up and the show times board was empty. Everywhere I went, I found nothing, and so I continued walking until I reached the beach, the only place left. Each step along the sand dunes felt dense as I waited for the slope to recede and the beach to present itself. The sky hung down on me in a way I knew what was coming before I saw it – a great vast emptiness of cloud, drizzle, and beach. Not a soul, not a head beneath a wave, or a rainbow umbrella to lie under.

# SIMON EAGLE

'But mister, can't we just look at this stuff online?' said Benjamin, the fourteen-year-old in the thirteen-year-old class, and Simon Eagle, looking around him, tried to think of a way to explain the value of experiencing art. The cabineted items and filled frames remained silent, looking in every direction but his own.

'How about you have a look around and come back to me in ten minutes if you're still struggling.' He paused to clear his throat behind a loosely clenched fist. 'You might even find something you like.'

Benjamin didn't seem to have listened, and to the tune of his tapping feet, said, 'Mr Eagle, are you bored? You look bored.'

Simon smiled the kind of smile that didn't reach his eyes, wishing the suggestion away.

'But are you?' Benjamin said, adding, 'your cheeks are all red.'

'No, I'm not,' Simon replied, still trying to smile. 'Now look, it's not often we get out of the classroom and get to look around a gallery. Let's make the most of it.'

Benjamin flung his arms out and pretended to fly away.

Simon's cheeks were very pink. He knew the conversation had been loud enough that his supervising teacher, Mrs Lee, had overheard. He also knew Mrs Lee wasn't the sort of person to let the interaction drift away without commentary.

'Everything okay over here, Simon?'

Mrs Lee liked to call him Simon to remind him that not only did he belong to the generation where it was becoming steadily acceptable to call teachers by their first names, but also that she was much older than him, and therefore ranked higher in most categories (wisdom, experience, loneliness, and the rest).

Simon nodded. 'Yes, thanks Mrs Lee.'

He had made the mistake of calling her Anne during his first week under her supervision. They had been standing in the staff room, stirring granules of instant coffee into Luminarc glass mugs. In response she had given her coffee a slightly brisker stir than usual, and later during class wrote her name in capitals on the whiteboard, underlining it, MRS LEE, even though they were well into the year and the whole school knew her name better than their own.

'It's nearly eleven,' she twisted her watch so that its face was recentred. 'How do you feel about distributing the worksheets soon? Then we'll break for lunch around twelve-thirty, gather everyone to chat about the exercise after they've eaten.'

The worksheet was divided into four sections. The first asked the students to select an item from the exhibition. Then for the second, explain why they chose it. Third, how it made them feel. Fourth, why it made them feel that way. It seemed like an easy enough activity, but when Mrs Lee had emailed it to Simon for feedback the day before, he had stared into the spaces between the answer lines as if they were asking too much of him. And that feeling had not lifted, had stayed with him through the evening as his boyfriend asked if they had enough money to book a holiday; was there in the morning when the alarm entered his dreams as the sound of a fire engine; was still there when he entered the gallery, and decided he did not love art the way he used to.

⚘

Simon was seventeen the first time he set foot inside a gallery. Most kids from the city grew up going to galleries much younger – on weekends with parents, or on regular school field trips. But when his parents passed away, he'd been carted up the coast to Waikanae, one of the region's small towns, where his grandparents lived. There isn't a lot to say about Waikanae. Simon thinks of it as a nice place, but the sort of nice that doesn't do you many favours. Like an idle friend on Facebook, or a lost item of clothing. So, when his Art History teacher decided it was time for the class to catch the southbound train to the city, Simon had not known what to expect, and so he expected nothing. He sat on the bus and watched Waikanae peel away, with its few stores that remained open like leftovers, the New World supermarket that people passing through liked to call the Small World, and the signature Liquorice Café that marked the beginning of the motorway with its fake allsort nailed to the roof. He thought about his Opa's scabby arms, and he thought about what to get him for his birthday. He lifted his hand and felt his way around the pimples protruding from his forehead. Later that day, standing in front of a painting of two naked men intertwined by a river, he brought his hand back up and picked one of the pimples until unripe pus and a small dot of blood was released.

After this, galleries and museums seemed to appear fortuitously. The funeral home for his Opa happened to be a block from the national museum, which he visited before and after the ceremony. His first flat in Tāmaki Makaurau neighboured the house of an art dealer who took a liking to him, until one afternoon they kissed and the dealer announced he was married, but gave him a framed painting to keep on his way out.

With a small chunk of inheritance from the subsequent passing of his Oma, Simon exchanged his second year at teachers' college for a university in London. Between classes, an unsteady boyfriend and an unsteady amount of sleep, he found himself walking through the galleries of the city. Pimples and hairline receding, he looked at sweeping sculptures and blockbuster exhibitions of Monet and Gauguin. He eyeballed the Rex Whistler mural between mouthfuls of cake. He even took himself to the Tate bathroom to masturbate, just once, overcome by the beauty of it all.

He continued through the year until it was time to return to New Zealand, and while he moved through the tides of his twenties and their many blind corners, he knew that every time he mustered the energy to walk through the entrance of a building with art inside, he would be okay. The dial of the existentialist world inside him would slowly make its way up the warmth scale.

🔻

And yet here he was, adrift from the spell he so badly wanted to rely on. What was going on inside his mind? Many things. His own gallery of happenings. At the entrance hung a video installation of his boyfriend waiting for him to say something, playing on repeat. Then, to the right, the garbage bin he was supposed to take out yesterday morning. Above that, a framed collage of various screenshots (a low-hanging bank account balance, clickbait headlines that frustrated him, an unopened message from an ex). On a pillar in the middle was a journal he wrote when he was coming out in high school. On an identical pillar next to it, the journal he kept when he began teaching, closed for symbolic reasons. After this, the items got more abstract – a lurching clay sculpture covered in acidic neon paint, a large penis erupting with lava, the outline of a gravestone dug into the floor, a vial of tears, a keg of sweat.

🔻

Benjamin sat in the corner, folding his worksheet into a paper plane. After three rocky flight attempts, he unfolded it and began to draw birds in the white spaces. Everyone around him was moving their pencils lightly across the paper, making answers. The questions didn't make sense to him. The letters switched places and played with him like a seesaw. But he needs to be on his best behaviour today, or so his sister had told him that morning while she cut sandwiches into triangles and put them in a plastic bag. Still, what did best behaviour mean to him? For the trip to the zoo, he had been the best at getting the teachers to laugh when he said the capybaras looked like hamsters pumped full of ice cream. He'd also been pretty good at getting the gorillas to swing their arms around as though they were dancing, and had even managed to get one of the hyenas to race him, kind of. On Athletics day, he had decided the only competition he wanted to partake in was the vortex throw. When it came time to push it into the sky and across the field, he accidentally hurled it into a gust of wind, which carried the rubber toy into the long jump sandpit. During the Year 10 pantomime competitions, Benjamin forgot the pre-rehearsed dance his class opened with and so he wiggled his hips and swung his arms around in a quiet sort of way, hoping no one would notice, but everyone did.

'Benjo, what're you up to over here?'

Demetri sat himself down, pushing his bum up against the wall.

'Not a lot,' Benjamin replied, playing with his shoelaces.

'You gonna do something funny today? Suuuuurely.' Demetri shuffled over to Benjamin until he was close enough to whisper, 'how about you go stick your finger up the nose of that statue?'

Benjamin looked over at the statue with its creamy grey limbs and cherub face.

'Na, gross. It's naked.'

'It's not actually naked. It would have to be human to be naked. But it's not. It's concrete. Would you call the floor naked just 'cause it doesn't have clothes on?'

'Guess not,' Benjamin mumbled.

'Bro, are you really scared of a statue?'

And so, Benjamin got up from the floor and walked over to the statue, surveying the nook of the gallery they were in to check no one was around. He stuck his finger into the nose and felt around the smooth hole of cold stone. The nostril wasn't large enough for him to get more than the length of a fingernail in. He looked back at Demetri to check he'd seen, then up at the statue, into its marble eyes. They looked back at him blankly. He took his finger out and looked down at his shoes. He half expected a teacher to appear and reason with him, 'Benjamin, what about the statue's feelings?'

Demetri clapped him hard on the thigh when he sat back down. Benjamin picked his worksheet back up off the floor and returned to an unfinished sketch of a sparrow. They sat in silence for a moment. Then Demetri said, 'Okay, now I dare you to go find Mr Eagle and pull that pink button off his shirt.'

Benjamin did not break eye contact with his worksheet. The owl in the bottom right corner had different sized eyes, and the sparrow looked more like a pigeon. He scrunched the sheet up into a tight ball. Then, he stood and wandered around the bend, past a group of students discussing a music video, until he found Simon sitting on a bench in front of a line of portraits.

Benjamin threw his scrunched-up worksheet into Simon's face. It seemed to take them both by surprise. Benjamin's mouth turned into a small 'o', while Simon pulled his shoulders back, his single earring rocking back and forth with the movement.

Then, quite suddenly, Benjamin sat down next to Simon.

'I'm sorry I threw that paper at you, mister.'

'It's okay,' Simon said sadly, 'but you've got to stop doing stuff like this. You could get in real trouble if Mrs Lee saw you.'

'But I wouldn't throw it at Mrs Lee,' he replied, picking the paper ball up from the floor and stuffing it into his back pocket.

Simon hesitated for a moment. He looked at Benjamin's lips, which were cracked but at the same time slathered in saliva. Simon thought they were a peculiar shape, thin at the edges and a little lumpy in the join. Then the lips said, 'Are you okay?'

'Me? Yeah, I'm fine. Are you okay?'

'Yeah, I'm fine too. Hey mister, I was wondering,' he closed and opened his mouth again, 'why do you wear that pink button on all your shirts?'

Simon hesitated again. 'They're, they're my mother's. I found them in her old sewing kit. So I sew them on my shirts as a sort of…' he paused to pedal his hands through the air, 'connection.'

'Oh, that's cool. Do you have a partner, Mr Eagle?'

There was something in the question that both softened

## SIMON EAGLE

Simon and made him feel hard-edged. The heart of a lamington.

'You can't really ask questions like that, Benjamin. But yes, I do have a partner.'

'Is it a boy or a girl?'

That's a question for married couples who throw baby showers, Simon wanted to say. 'A boy,' he said instead.

'Is that why you wear the pink button?'

'No. Well yes, and no.'

They stared at the ground for a while, avoiding eye contact with one another.

'Hey, Mr Eagle?'

'Yes, Benjamin?'

'I know I'm meant to do it myself, but do you reckon you could help me with that worksheet? The letters, they've been—' he moved his left hand in the air as though patting an imaginary basketball, '—jumping around.'

Simon leafed through his binder until he found a spare worksheet, then fished a pen out from his satchel.

'Okay, well first things first, choose a piece of art from the gallery.'

'Them,' Benjamin said, pointing towards the closest portrait. Inside the frame was a seated woman in a thick black dress, who looked tired, loosely holding the hand of a young girl, who looked angry. Simon stood to check the title card beneath the frame and jotted down *unidentified woman and child, woman holding child's hand.*

'Okay then, why'd you choose this one?'

'It's in front of us.'

Simon raised his eyebrows.

'Well… the frame is nice too. Very gold.' He paused to see whether the answer was enough, and after a few beats of silence, quickly added, 'And there's that tiny note in the woman's hand, so I guess that's kind of interesting. It's like it could be some kind of special secret.'

Simon scribbled something down. 'Nice work. Look, we're already halfway. Third question. How does it make you feel?'

Benjamin closed his mouth, fumbling around with something inside him. 'Can't you do this one for me, mister?'

Simon paused, fumbling around with something inside of him, too. He looked into the eyes of the older woman, felt the ache of her shoulders and the weight of the letter in her palm. Benjamin peered at the small girl, felt the scowl in her brows and the empty grasp of her mother.

'How about I list off some emotions and you choose one?' Simon said.

'Okay.'

'Happy. Sad. Scared. Angry. Excited. Curious. Any of those stand out?'

'I guess.'

'Which one?'

'All of them.'

Simon took the pen back to the worksheet.

'Okay. And why does it make you feel that way?'

Benjamin stood up then, walked so close to the frame that Simon wondered if he would have to tell him to step back. But Benjamin turned to walk back to the bench, and once seated, said, "'Cause they look just like me and you.'

Simon felt his eyebrows relax. Something very small had shifted inside him. It could have been his breakfast making its way somewhere more comfortable, but in that moment, he decided it was the sort of sensation that people find difficult to name. He could remember a few times he had felt it – like when he received a hug from a girl called Kirana who lived next door to him in Waikanae. They were six and he had just stubbed his toe and cried out for help. Then there was the ride back from his first party in the city, when he looked out the window at the Kapiti Coast and felt the ocean was opening up to him. There was a hazy collection of the days he woke with nothing more than a desire to watch whatever was going on outside his window. He remembered the walks he took with his Oma along the beach, discussing what to do with the week ahead of them. It was a peculiar game, this act of retrieval. No matter where he put his attention, nothing ever looked the same as it once did. So as Simon looked down at Benjamin biting his nails, his thoughts ballooning as he considered the portraits within himself, within Benjamin, the them within everyone and the everyone within them – he wondered if this would be one of the moments he would take with him.

Then, a shuffle of footsteps, the chorus of students clicking their pens, a glide of the automatic doors, and the shrill of Mrs Lee's voice saying it was time for lunch. But before standing to help usher students out into the foyer, he jotted something down on Benjamin's worksheet, folded it up, and handed it to him.

# TWINNING

The game we richies play nowadays to keep us occupied is called *Separated Twins*. In it, we are flown into an unknown location with two pictures of our target's faces. They're identical twins, separated at birth and discarded to opposite ends of the wealth spectrum. It's meant to show how money plays a role in defining privilege, but the only people that can afford to play the game are loaded, and I guess the poor don't really need convincing, do they? Basically, whoever invented it didn't realise they'd just created a travelling board game, a theme park for the affluent and bored.

It's only once we've been able to jostle them into the same place, and get them to look at each other, in the flesh, that the level has been completed. Some twins are more fun to find than others. Last year I perused over thirty strip clubs in Miami on a quest to find Krystle Jones, and then twenty country clubs in

Maryland searching for her twin, Camilla Wright. I plunged headfirst into the hedonistic extremes of the world, and it was delicious. Other times, it takes too long and gets tiresome.

The strangest part, and my favourite, is figuring out how to get them close enough to see each other. It's more complicated than you think. Trying to convince a Moscow socialite and a Tolyatti factory worker to enter the same café, let alone the same general vicinity, can be near impossible. I think that's meant to be the whole point. Broaden the players' understanding of the vastness of the gap or whatever.

Anyway, I'm going to tell you about the latest level. I got dropped into New Zealand! Of all places. At first, I had no idea where I was. I'd once hopped on a treadmill and selected my VR surroundings to be Auckland city, and it was all grey buildings and green bush. Nothing looked particularly old, or new, just ugly. But nothing in this level looked like anything I'd seen of Auckland. I pivoted left and right while I waited for the country to reveal itself. There were two large paddocks filled with hairy cows, a spindly sort of fence separating them from me, the chirp of some kind of summertime insect, and a sign behind me that read Bulls, 3 kilometres. I turned back to the cows. 'Are you bulls?' I said, only half-joking, but they just moaned their moos in reply. The longer I walked down the road, the more signs I saw. They all said BULLS, used the same thick black font, and included a pun (*Herd of Bulls? A Town Like no Udder*) along with the number of kilometres remaining. There was the faint smell of manure, a large parking lot filled with portable homes, and the distant trickle of a river keeping me company. Soon enough I reached the town centre, which was really just two motorways stretching out their fingertips, locking into a pinkie promise that consisted of a café (*delect-a-bull*), a town hall (*soci-a-bull*), a pub (*drink-a-bull*), a library (*read-a-bull*), and four or so rubbish bins (*response-a-bull*).

'Where am I?' I murmured to myself, standing at an obsolete traffic light.

'You're in Bulls,' someone said from behind me.

I turned around. He was small, maybe eleven, leaning against one of the rubbish bins. Looked a bit like a farm boy. Skinny arms, scruffy hair, friendly face. He was wearing a singlet and what looked like a pair of board shorts.

'Bulls where?' I asked – if you're good at Separated Twins then you know the first thing to do is befriend someone, a local, anyone who can act as a sort of guide.

He looked at me strangely. 'New Zealand.' He lifted his hands high in the air before exclaiming 'BULLS' as though he were saying BOO, then giggled to himself.

I pulled the pictures from my back pocket and lifted one up. She looked forty-ish, no older than me. Wide-set eyes, thin mousy hair, oval face, two piercings, full lips. 'Do you know who this woman is?' I asked the boy.

'Eh?' he said.

'Do you know who this is?' I tapped the picture.

'Looks tuh me like that lady who stole Boyo's truck.'

Bingo. 'Do you know her name?'

'Maybe it's Kitty.'

'Kitty.'

'She's in prison.'

'Prison for what?'

'Dunno, Boyo's truck. Or sumthin else.'

I lifted the second picture up – her face identical, only slightly more... firm? Healthier, well fed but also well exercised, and her hair was styled neatly, no piercings. 'What about this woman?'

'That's the Prime Minister's daughter.'

Too easy, I thought to myself. It usually took me at least a few weeks of meandering to come across someone that knew just one of them.

'What prison is Kitty in?' I asked.

'That one,' the boy said, pointing at nothing in particular, the *delect-a-bull* café in the way.

'And the Prime Minister's daughter? Where does she live?'

'Auuuckland, I think.' A truck chugged past, then its brakes screeched on.

'How far's Auckland from here?'

'What's your name?'

'Calvin,' I replied.

'Fancy.'

'Not really. How far?'

'Aaaaaaages away,' the boy said. He looked quite pleased with himself. 'You'll be on the bus for eteeeeernity. That's what Dad says. That bus takes an eteeeeeernity.'

# *TWINNING*

I laughed, decided it was time I asked the boy what his name was. But before I got the chance, he looked up at me, quite seriously, and said 'So, what are you doing tonight?'

'Sorry?'

'Tonight. Will you come round for dinner?'

It was always risky befriending children. Sometimes, they mislead you. Other times, strict parents get in the way of them guiding you. I'd had a particularly bad run-in with a kid's mother after she discovered us walking through the outskirts of Vondelpark together. Can't blame her. But the level had stretched across months, and I'd grown tired of asking strangers on the streets of Amsterdam for help only to get ignored. Children are often the most curious, the most interested in helping. But now I have a strict no-guide rule for kids that want to just *hang out*.

'Alright, bud. It was nice chatting.' I started walking away. For a moment, I considered hiring a car. Taking the back roads on my way to the prison. Or was every road a back road here? The only thing I knew about New Zealand was sheep. More sheep than people. Did they have a town called sheep, too? I tried to think of sheep puns, but could only come up with baaaa-ber.

'Where you going?' the boy asked.

'To the pub,' I replied. Somewhere he couldn't follow me.

'Alright,' and with a hop and a skip, he was walking beside me. 'Only one pub here. The Rat Hole.'

'Drink-a-bull?' I joked. By the time I'd said it, we were standing outside. The boy didn't even flinch as I swung through the pub's front door – just stepped straight in.

'Pete!' the bartender chirped. 'Thought you'd gone sober.'

Christ, the little boy used to drink. I looked straight down at him and shook my head. He looked straight back up at me, eyes open wide.

'He's sober,' I said. 'Don't you worry.'

'Now that would be something to worry about,' the bartender chuckled.

I nodded, pulled up a seat.

'Beer, please.'

The boy, Pete, clambered up onto the stool next to mine, rested his chin on the edge of the bar while I watched my pint being poured.

I looked around for clues – people or items that could deliver information on the twins to me quickly. It was normally a fruitless mission, but something I was in the habit of doing. All I could see was a pub. Clock said it was eleven in the morning. Two of the four gambling machines were in use. Somebody, out of sight, was muttering something about the way their cows had started reacting to the rain. There was a woman in the far corner counting coins. A fly droned above us in lazy circles. I looked back at the bartender, who was scraping froth from my glass. He had a thick chin, like it had been knocked permanently swollen. Pete, still next to me, looked bored.

The bartender passed me my drink. I took a long sip, then pulled the pictures out from my pocket, slid the image of the poorer one across the bar. 'Do you know what prison this woman's in?' I asked him.

'Oh, Kit,' he sighed.

'She a local?'

'Yeah,' he said, looking at me like it was common knowledge. I shrugged. 'You know, local this, local that,' he continued. 'Lived out in Tangimoana. Came in often, so local enough.'

'What'd she do to get locked up?' I took another sip of beer.

'Stole a truck—'

'Boyo's truck!' the boy interjected, bouncing a little in his seat.

'And rammed it into the gassy out in Sanson. High as a kite, 'parently. Not like her, but she had that two-year-old at home, and her guy was getting all rowdy, and well,' he brought his lips into his mouth, 'you know how it goes.'

'Sheesh,' I said, feigning sympathy. 'And what prison is she in, do you know? Might pay her a visit.'

'That's a nice idea. Gotta be in Arohata, I believe.'

I nodded. The bartender lingered a few odd moments, as if waiting for me to say something more, before disappearing into a backroom and returning with a cardboard box filled with packets of crisps and began stacking them into a shallow wicker basket near the lines of spirits.

🔱

Rental car, that was the first thing on my mind. No other plan had clearly formulated itself, other than to put the PM's daughter on the backburner while I scoped out the prison for possible reasons to hoax her into a visit. No point in arriving in Auckland without ammunition. The boy, of course, tried to come with me.

'Don't you have school to go to?' I asked him.

'It's Sunday,' he said, trailing behind me.

Touché. 'Any rate, I can't be taking you with me without your parents knowing.'

'Na-uh,' he replied. 'Dad likes it when I go out and do stuff. Then you can come for dinner, no problem.'

I walked on, away from the centre of the township, ignoring the sounds of his footsteps behind me. Every so often, cars whooshed by along the motorway, on their way someplace else. It was a stop-off town, I was gathering. A fill your tank, fill your stomach sort of place. I passed the tourist centre (*inform-a-bull*), and then the police station (*const-a-bull*), before finally setting my sights on an auto centre (*drive-a-bull*). I stepped inside, the bell above the door jingling at my arrival. Behind a desk covered in papers and three coffee cups was a balding woman working her way down a piece of paper with a yellow highlighter. Above her, a wonky fan made its rounds, playing with what was left of her hair.

'Morning,' I said. She looked up at me, then over at the boy.

'Morning, Pete,' she replied, then returned to her highlighting.

Clearly everyone knew the boy. I gestured for him to sit with me. 'Need a car,' I said. 'Got any I can rent for the day?'

She looked up again, squinted her eyes at me. She wasn't unfriendly looking, but she was suspicious, and a little scary. 'This is what I can help you with,' she said as she handed me a flyer, then ran her highlighter along another line. The flyer read vehicle servicing inspections, car repairs, WOFs.

'Do you know where I can rent a car?'

'Closest is Palmy.'

'Palmy?'

'Palmerston North.'

'Right.' I looked at the boy for inspiration. He looked back at me, cheekily. 'And you can't, like, call in a favour for me and this little guy? Surely there's someone about town that has a car they don't need for the day?'

The woman leant back in her croaking seat. 'I suppose I could lend you my Subaru, but it'll cost you.'

'Name your price.'

'Four-hundred bucks.' She smirked.

I smirked back. I always loaded my *Separated Twins* credit card with at least a few hundred thousand dollars, plus I kept a wad of cash in most currencies. Never know when you're going to get stuck somewhere for too long. 'It's a done deal,' I said, and held out my hand.

Her eyes widened, then she squinted at me again. 'Don't know what you're playing at,' she said slowly, and stood to get her keys. Didn't even make me sign a contract.

᛭

Driving along State Highway 1, 'I'm on Fire' by Bruce Springsteen blasting through the radio, windows cracked an inch, I felt what I always felt once a level got going, a rising anticipation in the chest, akin to what I'd imagine PhD students feel when their research finally locks into place and revelations are on the near horizon. I was happy to see the backs of those puns and the emergence of regular transport signs – *Levin, 55km. Otaki, 75km. Wellington, 150km*, but then the boy got in the way of my moment by lifting his feet onto the dashboard and singing along with the wrong lyrics: *Hey lil diddle is your caddy home? Did he go and leave you on your own? MmmMMMmmm I got a bad cheshire…*

Never liked kids, if you couldn't tell already. Carrie, my ex-fiancée, had wanted children. We were all fun and loose at the beginning – partying till the crack of dawn and doing whatever we pleased with our hangovers. Then something changed, something I wasn't privy to, and her face stopped lighting up at the thought of a Campari Spritz at three in the afternoon, but instead at little squirming babies in strollers passing us on the street. It turned out she'd actually been pregnant (that was the change!), but she only told me once she'd had a miscarriage. All downhill from there. It was the last relationship I had with anyone. After that, it was just me and Separated Twins. I was going to play it till I died. I was on level thirty-four.

*Ohhhh OHHHH Ohhhh I'm on fire,* the boy continued, howling up at the sagging roof of the woman's Subaru. Trees whipped by around us, small crosses decorated in plastic flowers appearing on most corners of the road to mark crash-caused-deaths. The old GPS screen showed a pixelated vehicle making jagged progress on a thick grey road. I liked the feeling of the gas pedal beneath my shoe, the motor vibrating through it and up into my calf. I tried to picture Carrie's face, but all I could conjure were her features. There were her eyes, all glassy, and her lips, freckled at the top, below a cute nose. I held them there, in my mind, willing a full face to emerge, but it was replaced by Kitty's, piercings and all. We drove on.

*TWINNING*

⚜

When we pulled into the Arohata prison car park, the boy was asleep, and it was nearly 2:00pm. I left the doors unlocked and let him be. As I walked across the lot, I realised I'd never been to a prison. They had always existed in faraway places in my mind, on islands surrounded by a choppy ocean, or marooned far away from anything remotely urban, not plonked on the hilly edge of the highway, as this one was. I was surprised none of the separated twins had ever been incarcerated before, given the surely disproportionate amount of poor people that wound up in jail, and thought this really demonstrated progression in the game.

I looked up at the chain-link fence. With the highway behind me now, the main building looked odd, as though it had been put on its hill as an afterthought, a foreground of pine trees that made me feel I was somewhere in the Swiss Alps, and the prison ought to be stripped of its security, painted a pale pink, and transformed into some charming historical building recently refurbished as a mountain resort. I made my way to the front entrance and scuffed my feet while I looked into the eyes of the two security cameras. A beep registered my presence, and soon the door was shuddering open. I stepped inside and listened as the door closed once more, clicking into its lock before the secondary door began opening its mouth. Inside, a tired looking security officer stood leaning against an X-Ray machine.

'Shoes and belts off. Nothing in your pockets,' he droned. Above him, one of the fluorescent tube lights flickered on and off. Straight out of a detective film, I thought, and began sliding my belt out of the loops of my pants. Chucked my sneakers and my satchel bag in a tray, and wandered on through, past the rows of empty seats, to a woman inside a glass box.

'Visitor Application Form,' she said cheerily through her mic. She looked no older than thirty, dimples chirping out her cheeks.

'Can I have one to fill out?' I asked.

Her smile faded. 'No form, no visit.'

'I just got into the country today,' I said in what I hoped was a very sad voice. 'I'm here to visit my cousin. She's very dear to me, and I've flown all this way. Please, couldn't you just give me a blank form and I'll fill it out pronto?'

'Sorry, sir. Rules are rules. Forms go to the warden and the warden sends results back to you by mail. Takes weeks, man.' Her face softened again.

'Oh, damn,' I let out a fake groan, ran my hands through my hair, let them rest at an angle that said God, I'm so distressed. 'What if,' I leaned a little closer to the glass wall between us. 'What if I could give you some, you know?' I rubbed my thumb and index finger together. She looked over at the security guard, who had one eye closed, one eye trained on the television displaying a black-and-white carpark devoid of movement.

'How much we talking?' she whispered.

'How much you need?'

'Naw,' she sighed. 'You name your price, then I'll name mine.'

'Five hundred.'

She glanced back at the security guard. 'Two grand, you gotta deal.' Then she started looking worried again, like it was something she'd never done before.

'Like your style,' I said, hoping it might lighten up whatever apprehension was inside of her. It seemed to work – she smiled.

'Here's the form,' she whispered, then paused to think. 'When you slide it through the slot to me, fold the paper and wedge the cash inside.'

I sat down in one of the seats and began scribbling down my details. I realised I didn't know Kitty's surname, so I just wrote Kitty twice, and folded the sheet in half. Then I took my jacket off and bunched it around my waist so that I could shuffle the cash out of my satchel without being too obvious. Counted out twenty New Zealand $100 bills, all red and plasticky with a moustached man printed on them, and slid them into the gap between my folded form. When she took it from me, I think she realised she wouldn't be able to open it up right there and then to check all the details I'd written were right, she really was a raw dog at all this, and so she just whispered, 'Oi, who you visiting?'

'Kitty.'

'She know you're coming?'

'Ya-huh.'

A buzz rang through the room, and a door to the right opened. 'Guard, please escort him to the visitor's room and notify Kitty her guest's arrived.'

A man I hadn't noticed before stepped forward, gave me the once over, and gestured for me to follow him through.

The innards of the prison were confusing. Parts were new, gloriously shiny, then you turned a corner and found yourself walking along cracked concrete and linoleum again. There were cameras everywhere, and through the windows I could faintly make out a row of units that looked to be more like social housing than part of a prison compound, only they were wrapped in barbed wire.

'What're those smaller buildings for?' I asked the guard as we turned down another corridor.

'Self-care units. For the prisoners with medical issues, or the ones nearing the end of their sentence.'

We arrived at the visitor's room, and I sat in the seat the guard showed me to. 'Wait here,' he said. 'Five minutes.'

I waited. While I waited, I looked at the picture of Kitty some more. Hard eyes, raised red skin around each piercing, hair halfway dyed. There was still, or so I thought, something kind about her. Then the guard emerged with her in tow, and she looked at me with accusatory eyes. I gulped.

'Who are you?' she said, pulling back the chair opposite from mine. 'If you're one of Billy's friends, tell him he can get fucked.'

'I'm Calvin, not a friend of Billy's, don't know a Billy.'

'You're American.'

'How'd you know?' I tried my best to give her a charming smile, but she seemed unimpressed.

'What's the deal, then? You some kinda do-gooder Christian type?'

See, this is where it usually gets tricky. There are only three rules in *Separated Twins*:

*TWINNING*

1. *Separated Twins* holds no responsibility for a player's health and safety while they are in a level.

2. Upon entrance to the game, each player may only have the clothes they are wearing and one zipped bag containing cash, their ST credit card, and the two pictures they were given during level induction. All other items must be purchased within the level.

3. Player's may never reveal that they are playing a game. Doing so will result in immediate expulsion from *Separated Twins* and any affiliated games under the Entertainment Frequency label.

So, I couldn't exactly have said, 'Hey Kitty, I'm playing this game, and I need you to make an appeal to the media about a separated twin of yours who happens to be the Prime Minister's daughter and then make sure she comes and visits you.'

'Not Christian,' I said. 'But I do want to do good. I'm here as part of a mentorship programme.' This was good, I thought. I hadn't even planned it. 'It's organised by the Government.'

'Fuck the Government.'

'Well, not the Government,' I backtracked. 'Funded by it, I guess. But we're independent. We match young mothers in prisons with, um…' I stumbled a bit while I tried to think of a word other than affluent. 'Young mothers not in prison.'

'You mean rich people.' She leant back in her seat and folded her arms across her chest.

'Not exactly.'

'Sir, you rich?'

'No.'

'Seem pretty rich to me, the way you're speaking. The way you have time to do good.'

'I'm comfortable,' I replied. She raised her eyebrows. This was harder than I thought. Normally, I just found the poor twin and asked them if they'd like to join me for some kind of dinner, then scope out the rich twin's regular dining spots. The poor twin would be dubious, sure, a strange American man insisting on taking them out of their neighbourhood for dinner? Sometimes I'd had to go as far as to pretend I was an investor, interested in whatever they were doing for money – drycleaning or driving cabs or working a corner store – and that the dinner was actually a business meeting. Never felt as guilty about doing that as I should have, watching their face as they met their twin for the first time, confusion blooming, then the possibility of financial security leaving their face as I walked away. Anyway, there was no way I was getting Kitty anywhere. I decided I'd have to rethink my process for this one. Rich twin was the entrance point, apparently.

'Do I get any, like, good behaviour points if I do a programme like this?' Kitty asked.

'Oh, yes.'

'As in early release?'

'Yes.'

She eyed me suspiciously.

'Up to twenty percent of the sentence, depending on how the mentorship goes.'

'Up to?'

'Twenty percent.'

'Okay.'

'That's great,' I replied. 'Only thing you gotta do is write your mentor a letter. Haven't confirmed one for you yet, new sign-up and all, so just leave the addressee blank.'

I handed her a piece of paper and a pen. The Guard eyed us.

'What do I write?' she said, holding the pen in her left hand. It transformed her, somehow, into a child at school.

'Just the usual, introduce yourself. Explain why you're here and why you need a mentor, how you're excited for them to visit, the name of the prison, anything else of note.' What a fat load of garbage, I thought, but it seemed to work. She started writing.

🜍

By the time she'd finished, visiting hours were finishing; I figured it must be a long letter. The guard came over to us and said, 'Time's up, also, there's a young boy in the reception room waiting for you.'

Kitty raised her eyebrows at me. 'You got kids?' she said, surprised.

'No, babysitting.'

'Checks out,' she shrugged. 'You don't seem like a father to me,' and she handed me the letter and turned away.

Back through the maze I went, the guard annoyingly

clucking his tongue as we walked. When we reached the reception, the lady officer in the glass box looked slightly flushed in the cheeks and refused to make eye contact with me. The boy was slumped low in one of the chairs, pulling at a piece of thread that had come loose from his shorts.

'I'm starving,' he said. 'Can we please go home now so we can have dinner?'

🌟

'You're a bit strange, aren't you,' the boy said, back in his passenger seat, ocean gliding by outside his window, engine rumbling through the gas pedal and up my leg once again.

'Sure,' I replied, tapping the steering wheel along to the tune of a New Zealand country song I didn't know the words to.

'And you just turn up! Out of the blue!'

'Yeah.'

'It's a miracle really,' he sighed as though in a spell. He lifted his legs back up onto the dashboard.

We stopped off at a gas station. I bought the boy a bag of crisps to keep him going till his dinner, and a sausage roll for me. While I ate, pastry flakes floating all around me, I read Kitty's letter. It was shorter and less scrawly than I'd thought it'd be. The letters in every word looked carefully drawn, with measured space between each line and curve.

*Hi, nice to meet you. Name's Kitty. Bit weird I don't know yours. Pretty ashamed about what I've done, maybe we can talk about it together. Have a two-year-old called Tess. Love her, wish I wasn't in here so I could be a proper Mum to her.*

## TWINNING

*Have you ever done anything you're ashamed of?*

*My reckon is rich people do it all the time. Ain't no trucks crashing through windows or guns being pulled or meth being smoked, but plenty of that other stuff, in smaller doses, and with no consequences, so they get to throw the shame away easier. Maybe I'm wrong. Guess you can tell me. Name's Kitty Brown. Oh, I'm in Arohata Prison. Meet you soon.*

I immediately regretted not having supervised the writing of the letter. If this note arrived in my letterbox, I'd read it, find myself wildly confused, and disregard it. I certainly wouldn't be going to visit the prison. I decided to rewrite it myself, keep some of what she'd said, but formalise it, mention the programme and perhaps even make it sound like Kitty was requesting the PM's daughter specifically.

I got back into the car, hoped the boy might fall asleep again, but he just kept chitter-chatting.

'And Dad is so good at cooking fish. Sometimes I think it tastes like chicken. It's that good.'

'I thought kids were meant to hate their parents.'

'Na-uh. Dad's my best friend.'

'Just you wait till you're a bit older, son.' We drove through another small town, and I thought for a while about how that had been a weird thing for me to say. I don't think I'd ever called anyone son.

When we pulled back into Bulls, the auto centre was closed. I drove the car a few blocks before eventually pulling into an empty park near a garage painted with an adapted version of the American Gothic. I was reminded of the afternoon Carrie and I spent at the Art Institute of Chicago one winter, where she had stared at the original work so sadly, stuck looking at the expressions on the two farmers' faces, and the pitchfork in the man's hand. When I'd asked her what was up, she'd only shrugged and murmured something I couldn't hear.

The garage door version showed two Bulls standing upright in identical positions to the farmers, only the clothes and buildings in the background had a slight New Zealand twist to them I couldn't put my finger on, something run down about it, quirkier, and though they were wearing farmers clothes, their outfits seemed more light-hearted – the combination of the dungarees and spectacles on the male bull made him seem almost stoned, and their expressions looked eager. Something about it made me feel like I ought to laugh, but the laugh wasn't coming.

'You good to get home from here?' I asked the boy. I figured I'd go back to The Rat Hole and get myself some dinner, a beer, and rewrite this letter. Then I'd find somewhere to sleep and head off up to Auckland in the morning. Get myself a fake uniform with a fake organisation name printed on it and deliver the letter myself. I supposed I could bus, but really the intention to return the Subaru to that woman was dwindling. I'm no thief, but I'll happily push things past their return date.

'Na-uh,' the boy replied. 'You're coming for dinner, remember.'

'Look, I've got some things I need to sort.' I started walking in the direction of the bar, and, well, as you can probably guess, he followed me.

*TWINNING*

We sat in the same seats we'd sat in earlier that day, only this time the pub was about as full of drunkards as I imagined it could get. I asked the bartender, now a young woman in her early twenties with bleached hair, for a piece of paper, a pen, and a pint. I drank, then I wrote. Nothing I managed to craft seemed to hold any semblance of believability, but I kept trying. I ordered another drink. Then another. The boy swung his legs against the silver legs of the stool.

'When can we go for dinner? I'm hungry,' he moaned.

'Bud,' I sighed. 'Go home. Fun's over. I need to write.'

'Maybe I can help you.' Behind us, the door swung open, and a group of men in orange construction gear stumbled inside.

I looked down at what I had. Some trodden garbage on the organisation's purpose statement and fictionalised history – I'd decided to switch tact and write it from the 'CEO', followed by some preliminary information on the mentee candidate (Kitty) and some quote excerpts from her letter. When I re-read it, I just heard spam. Do not reply.

'You got any names for an, uh, organisation that does good for people in prisons?'

'Hmmm,' the boy leant back, giving it some serious thought. 'What about, like, Kindness or sumthin?'

Too weak, but the sentiment was there. The Kindness Programme was good. I nodded at him, ordered another beer and took a shot of tequila. Went straight to my head.

'Dinner time, dinner time, dinner time,' the boy chanted. His persistence for my company was something to be marvelled at.

'I don't know,' I answered, taking another large sip of beer.

'Think you should.'

I felt the edge of sadness. I'm not sure if it was the way Pete said it or if I was just drunk enough to be persuaded, but I eventually agreed to go with him.

We walked side by side in silence, the town cloaked in dusk, passing by homes that looked as though they'd just been unloaded onto land. No decorative features, no balconies. The whole town seemed to be taking a collective sigh.

Pete's house was as unassuming as the rest, just another timber box smattered with peeling paint. The beer had clearly taken effect because I stumbled my way up the plain concrete path, occasionally dipping off onto the dry grass.

'Wait here,' Pete said, and disappeared around the side of the house. I stood there, swaying without a breeze. This was getting embarrassing. Pete's father would see me, and either scream at me, or the boy for bringing a drunk man home. I turned to leave. Some situation I'd gotten myself into. A lawnmower growled to life from a paddock nearby. The fuck were people doing mowing lawns in the evening? Somewhere, a truck honked. Before I'd made it back onto the road, the front door swung open.

'Hello?' said a man's voice, not exactly disapproving. I kept my back to him, and continued walking.

'Oi!' he yelled. So I walked faster.

'Turn around,' he bellowed, and like a little boy being told off, I sheepishly turned around to face him. There, in the doorway, was what appeared to be my reflection. I blinked twice, waiting for his features to rearrange themselves into a face that didn't look identical to mine. But there was no way around it – he looked exactly like me.

🜚

Inside, he poured me a cup of tea. 'Who are your parents?' he asked. The boy stood by his side, innocent as ever. Their living room was plain. One dining table, two chairs, a framed picture of a shipwreck, a small box set television, and a fraying couch.

'I don't know,' I mumbled. It seemed all I was capable of saying now.

'And you're American?' he asked.

'Yes.' I could hardly look him in the eyes. 'I mean I think so.'

'You think so.' It seemed he was as dubious as I was. 'Are you drunk?'

'I think so.' I started to feel woozy. The heat flushed out of me. 'Get me out of here,' I said to the ceiling, hoping that somewhere, up there, the game-makers would hear me, and with a giant digital hand, pluck me out of whatever this was.

'Do you wanna glass of water?' the little boy said.

'Attaboy Eli,' the man replied.

'Eli? I thought his name was Pete.'

'No, I'm Pete,' the man replied, drawing his cup of tea closer to him.

I took a deep breath and tried to make sense of what was going on. And I'd be lying if I didn't tell you, the first thing that crossed my mind was how on Earth the boy had managed to afford to play my game. Secondly, well, I looked my twin in the eye, and blinked a few more times, as though he was something I'd conjured with my own imagination, as if it were good for such a thing.

# FAMILIAL REUNIONS

Daphne puts a piece of bread in the toaster but leaves it there, sitting in the vertical tray, until its spongy warmth has turned completely stiff. She looks at the empty kettle and wonders whether to fill it. Eventually deciding not to, she looks to the living room instead. There are two armchairs, one for her to sit in, the other to look at. The room is wrapped in faded floral wallpaper with small patches of vibrant cutouts where more furniture once stood. Her blood moves around her body like paste. She turns away from the living room and forgets why she's in the kitchen, seeing only small pockets of light come through the blinds and land on different appliances. The lifeless ding dong of the doorbell drifts in from behind her. She has forgotten that her grandson, James, is coming to Dunedin and that she, his grandmother, is housing him while he's here.

🞈

Meanwhile, Daphne's only daughter and James's mother, Lori, is in Tauranga – staring out the window and drumming her fingers against the kitchen island. She's considering how to dispose of the three hours ahead of her before her shift at the hospital starts – and with numerous tasks and a heady need to feel as if she's accomplished something – she has instead found herself stuck. She is not lazy, but whenever the moment appears, a ninety-nine percent decision about to boil over into three digits, something in her likes to pat it back down. No, there must be something more important than pruning the lime tree. No, listing items on Trade Me is a task teeming with sub-tasks and will require at least a full day if to be done in one go. She lets her pinkie close the drum and resists the urge to lift her index and begin the rhythm once more. Then, she lifts the fruit bowl by a centimetre to free the list of tasks beneath that her book club friends have devised as distractions:

Prune the lime tree

Meditate!

~~Pickle some cucumbers~~

Try yoga (call Helen if you want that free trial)

Write down feelings (regularly)

~~Get James to visit Daphne~~

~~Spring clean~~

Sell stuff on Trade Me

Vacuum the curtains

This is what their book club sessions are all about – improvised therapy peppered in between comments on the parts of the book they've actually managed to read.

Just last week, when Lori segued from discussing the first chapter of Where'd You Go, Bernadette, which included distracted comments on suitable nicknames (incl. Bernie, Bern, Dette, Dettie, Bee) to issuing an elevated distress order – announcing her mother was going to be admitted to a dementia care home, that she didn't have enough leave to visit before she was transferred, and eventually crying as she explained James refused to go, let alone leave his bedroom – they said, 'Let's make you a list, lists help everything.'


Lori eventually commits to pruning the lime tree. Pruning feels like an easy win. How could she lose at pruning? While she clips at the branches with a rusted pair of shears, Lori imagines she's cutting away at her fears.

—What if my mother dies before I can afford to get her into a care facility, snip.

—James is never going to leave his room, *snip*.

—Because of this, James will never really live a full life, *snip*.

—No first love, first job, first house, *snip*.

—Living with me until the end of time, *snip*.

—Or until we're all swallowed by a digital black hole, *snip*.

—I will never have enough money to retire, *snip*.

—What I've done is worse than all of this combined, *snip*.

The tree wobbles in the breeze, naked.

Lori turns to go back inside.

See, the James standing on the doorstep, waiting for Daphne to remember that ding dong means let me in, isn't James. Lori tried her hardest, she did, but nothing could get the Real James to budge.

'Why don't you go and stay with your grandma in Dunedin,' Lori had gently proposed. 'She needs company, and it's beautiful down there this time of year.'

He wasn't aware of it, but she was being sincere. But instead of imagining the trip – moments of warmth in the same house he had once visited as a baby, landscape sceneries of the Otago Peninsula coated in various sunsets – he only heard criticism, like a grey cloud coming out of his mother's mouth, emitting a barrage of potential assessments – that he was a failure, that she no longer wanted him under her roof, that he was a disappointment. So he furrowed his eyebrows and began to look mean.

'It smells bad in here,' Lori said. 'Open a window.' Then, she opened it for him. Noise from the outside world trickled in – a chain ticking from a neighbour's bicycle, squeals as small children ran through a cold water sprinkler – and still, James didn't break eye contact with the screen in front of him, at the millions of pixels that made up his alter-ego, no-name-hidden72, rotating in edit mode, and made only grunt noises in response until his mum walked away.

He has this to partly blame for the way Lori took his absence of a no as an opportunistic yes and wheeled a suitcase in.

## FAMILIAL REUNIONS

'I'll come and visit soon,' she said. 'Your grandma's really going to appreciate this.'

Pew, pew, pew, his pixelated gun went.

▲

When the day arrived for him to go, James locked his door until his flight had safely departed without him. Lori spent most of the morning seated on the hallway floor outside his bedroom, picking at the pilling carpet, begging him to reconsider.

'Jay-Jay,' she said, knocking on the door. 'Please come outside so we can talk this through.' When he didn't respond, she whispered, 'This is getting out of hand,' to herself, just loud enough that he could hear.

Inside his room, James was in bed, tangled in unwashed sheets that smelt of mildew and dog hair.

'We can still make it if we leave now,' she pleaded.

James, with his face tucked into his chin, stared at the screen in front of him, watching as no-name-hidden72 ran over a hill with slow robotism towards a large mound of ice, to which his character began to hack at it with a pick until a bonus item appeared above its head.

'Gran would really love to see you.'

He turned the volume of the computer game up until the crunch of no-name-hidden72's footsteps were blaring, the bonus item now successfully in his inventory, and Lori's voice was nothing more than a background hum.

▲

'Am I a bad mother?' Lori asked her book club, looking around the room with eyes that seemed to sweat.

'No, don't be silly,' said Tania, who was all teeth and had brought a packet of Tim Tams for them to share while they discussed *Eleanor Oliphant is Completely Fine* on Lori's patio.

'You're the boss,' said Caitlin the straight-shooter with the thick-rimmed glasses and foam platform shoes.

'Totally,' slightly-Catholic Miriam nodded.

'This is a disaster,' Lori said, wiping her nose against the sleeve of her cardigan. She looked at the lime tree, all branch no leaf, then fixed her gaze on the group once more. 'It's all stacking up,' she whimpered. 'And I can't do anything to fix it. My mother's all alone, I genuinely can't remember the last time James left his bedroom except to use the bathroom, and to top it all off,' she looked at the lime tree once more, it looked so sad, all hacked at, 'I'm just as alone as they are.' Then, she started sobbing – really sobbing, great gulps of air that did nothing but exacerbate the emotional overflow further.

'Oh Lori,' they hushed in unison, 'it's okay.'

'There, there. Things get worse before they get better. It's all going to be okay,' Tania said as she rubbed circles around Lori's back.

'And remember, you've got your list. You've got us. We've got you,' said Helen, the psychologist-turned-teacher.

'Alright,' said Caitlin after the suitable amount of quiet sympathy had passed, removing her glasses and lightly slapping her hands against her thighs, 'let's make a plan.'

## FAMILIAL REUNIONS

This was how it always seemed to go. When Miriam suspected her husband was cheating on her, Caitlin had instigated a complex investigation into his fidelity, including trailing his car home from work on multiple occasions, only to discover he had started habitually spending upwards of two hours parked along the Southern Coast to either read or write poetry. The day Tania announced she was too nervous to ask for a promotion, Caitlin had organised a schedule of meeting rehearsals, each with their own do or die scenarios – 'What if he says, the market conditions are too bad right now – what will you say? How will you say it!'. She had even crafted her own plan of attack mere minutes after breaking down and admitting she'd found out her daughter was seriously considering not having children:

A) Volunteer for crèche on Sundays to get baby fix

B) Plant baby reminders in daughter's house, e.g. novels with positive birthing stories

C) Encourage daughter's friends that have babies to explain perks of motherhood

They joked it was Caitlin's PR background coming to fruition, but no one doubted she'd emerged from the womb with the same decisive expression on her face.

'Have you thought about hiring a fake James?' Caitlin asked.

Lori's tears subsided for a moment. 'What?' replied Lori.

Caitlin shrugged. 'Students will do anything for a bit of cash.'

'Isn't that a bit twisted?' slightly-Catholic Miriam interjected. 'A fake grandson for a dementia-ridden grandmother doesn't seem entirely ethical,' and she let out a nervous tinkly laugh as she looked around the group for signs of agreement.

Caitlin paused, then stared up at the ceiling as though enquiring with God. When she brought her attention back to the group, a decision had been made. 'It's only twisted if you let it be,' she said with startled enthusiasm. 'This is no normal situation, and so normal solutions won't cut the mustard. Think of it this way: your mum gets company until you're able to visit, you can help Real James get out of the house, and soon enough you'll be with her. Fake James will get the boot. Real James will come with you. And she'll be none the wiser.'

GRANDSON WANTED

*Fixed-term contract*

I'm seeking a reliable young man between the age of nineteen to twenty-two years to fill in for my son for a one-week trip, starting as soon as possible. I need someone who can make my mother who is living with dementia (your temporary grandmother) feel loved and not alone. Cooking and cleaning are a plus. Her house is in Dunedin, so a student living in that area would work well. If this sounds like you, please send a cover letter outlining how you treat/treated your grandparents, along with the application below.

Selecting the right grandson for the job was easier than Lori thought it would be – only four people applied. The successful applicant was a twenty-one-year-old commerce student called Ryan. The picture he included showed him smiling in a sports uniform, standing on a rugby pitch, gleaming with a mixture of rain and sweat.

## FAMILIAL REUNIONS

'Noah sounds like a lovely boy,' Miriam said. They were sitting around the dining table at Lori's, taking turns reading each of the applications.

'Personally, I think Elijah sounds perfect,' Caitlin countered. 'He even volunteers for a retirement home.'

'This Toby boy barely wrote more than a sentence for each of the sections,' Tania sighed.

'What about Ryan?' Lori asked.

His application was nowhere near as well written as Noah or Elijah's, but Lori couldn't take her eyes off the picture of him standing outside. His cookie-cutter sentences (I am writing to express my interest... My name is Ryan... I am reliable and manage my time well... I love my grandparents) were given a new light – bless him for trying, Lori thought. Look at that grass, that smile, such a boy. A real boy.

After her friends left, Lori called Ryan's references. She didn't explain what the job was, but simply asked questions about what he was like.

'Oh, Ryan's a good kid,' his rugby coach said simply. 'Works hard. Great at rugby. Good head on his shoulders, that one.'


Ryan, Fake James, is wondering whether he's at the right house. It's been a few minutes since he last pressed the ringer, and he's looking around him for signs of an old person's existence. He finds a tiny ceramic frog wearing a straw hat behind a pair of gumboots and presses down on the doorbell one more time.

'Hello?' Daphne's voice comes from somewhere inside.

'Hey Grandma,' Ryan says loudly. 'It's me, James.'

'James?' Her figure appears and begins to shimmy across the stained glass as she walks closer. 'Oh, James!' She opens the door, looks him up and down, then back up again, and eventually welcomes him in with a hug.

After being accepted for the job, Lori sent Ryan an email and six attachments for him to study. Included was a picture of Daphne the last time she'd seen her. Now, bending down to let himself into her hug, he's struck by just how old she feels. As though at any moment, her body might disintegrate into dust, like a moth.

'You've gotten so tall,' she smiles, and, bringing her hand against her shoulder, exclaims, 'you used to be up to here!' before affectionately patting his arm. 'Come inside.'

Once he's found the spare bedroom, Ryan dumps his bag, changes into a fresh T-shirt, and presses his finger into the floral bedspread, inspecting the firmness of the mattress beneath.

Back in the kitchen, Daphne opens the fridge to assess what's inside. 'How does roast pork for dinner sound, Jay-Jay?' she says, popping her head into the hallway.

Lori informed Ryan of his many nicknames (Jay-Jay, Jamesy, and sometimes, when Daphne's feeling a little forgetful, Jonny), but it still takes him a while to register where he is, and that Daphne is talking to him.

'That sounds great,' he replies, walking to join her in the kitchen, arms crossed against his chest. 'Have you had a nice day so far, Gran?'

'Oh, it's been good, not bad. I went to the post office to pick up a package from your Aunty Doris.'

'That's nice.'

'It was nice,' she smiles again. 'Then I had my hair done, and afterwards, I was going to go for a walk around the park, but the weather turned, and so I—' she stops mid-sentence. Ryan waits patiently, eyeing a tin with windmills and tartan print that reminds him of his childhood money box.

'Jay-Jay, is that really you? You look so different!'

'It's me!'

'Oh, Jay-Jay!' She goes to give him another pat on the shoulder. 'I was thinking of making roast pork for supper. Would you like that?'

᛭

Real James has his bedroom door locked and the curtains pulled. He hates his mother more than usual today. Something about the way she told him what a beautiful day it is outside, how great it would be if he could walk the dog, he could even stop by the shop and get some ice creams for the two of them, made his insides bristle. She has no idea that there's something larger at play here – that he isn't just simply addicted to video games, but actively protesting against the state of the world by refusing to participate in it. James likes to watch YouTube explainer videos that reinforce this internal argument. Even his room, a blizzard of unwashed clothes and dirty dishes, is its own revolt against what the world expects of him. Cavemen used to live worse than this – unshowered, among the dirt. When he yelled this to Lori through the closed door a few weeks ago, she'd just yelled back, 'Cavemen also used to walk places. They were connected to nature, not holed up inside all day.' He'd almost taken it on board and had even considered going for a walk around the nearby reserve. But when she knocked on his door to ask whether he'd talk to his grandma on the phone, he'd grunted in anger and hopped back into bed for the rest of the day.

🔻

Ryan is cutting into a piece of pale meat drenched in gravy, thinking about the outline Lori provided him of how Real James eats.

'When he was younger, gosh he was a sweet young thing, he abided by her manners – no elbows on the table, no licking plates, never eating with his mouth open, the usual. But it's been years since he last visited. And nowadays, she's a lot more lenient with casual eating, so don't be alarmed if she starts eating her dinner on the couch.'

When he licks his fingers, Daphne chuckles. 'Are you still hungry? she says. 'We've got some leftovers in the freezer if you are.'

'Oh, I'm good thanks,' he replies, swallowing his last mouthful, logging the tastelessness of the meat to the list of things he wants to tell his girlfriend over the phone once Daphne goes to bed.

'Best save some room for pudding,' she smiles. 'We'll have it with Deal or No Deal. How does that sound?'

🔻

That evening, the springs croak as Daphne sinks into her armchair. Ryan sits in the chair opposite, wondering what the cinnamon-like odour is he can smell on the ornamental cushions. A smug looking host with a gummy smile welcomes them to the show and brings an audience member on stage to select a shiny silver briefcase from a line of smiling women in slippery dresses.

'I don't see why they put those girls in such small outfits,' Daphne says. 'They must get so cold.' She's holding a small bowl of apple crumble with cream, and every time she dips the spoon in, it wobbles and clangs against the rim of the bowl. Lori had bought her weighted utensils during her last visit that help steady her hands, but Daphne seems to have forgotten them. A spoonful of crumbs and cream drops onto the carpet. Ryan goes to get a cloth from the kitchen.

When he returns, the TV has switched to ads, and a woman is running through the rain with an umbrella over her head. Daphne is lifting herself out of her seat and murmuring something about bringing the washing in before the rain gets it. She shuffles out of the room and out into the backyard. Ryan follows her.

'Gran, it's not raining. It's only the television!'

But it's too late, she's out of sight.

⁂

After showering, Ryan calls his girlfriend, Amy.

'The whole house smells funny.'

'Ryan,' Amy groans. 'You can't say stuff like that.'

In the background, he can make out the clicking of her pen, a habit of hers she has openly admitted only emerges when she doesn't like the conversation she's in, or if she feels there's someplace else she'd rather be.

'What? It's true.'

'It's only smell,' she replies. 'What's the woman like?'

'Smell I have to live in. She's all good.'

'Is she nice? I love the smell of my grandparent's house. It's like, really old book pages, or baked cookies, but the cookies have been eaten hours ago.'

'I dunno if my grandparents' house smelt of much,' he replies. 'And yeah, she's nice. Still weird though.'

'World's gonna be weird if you take weird jobs.'

'Isn't every job a weird job? If you think about it long enough.'

'This is different. This is particularly weird. Leave off your CV weird. Moral compass jeopardised by money weird.'

'I am moral.'

'It's weird.'

'Sometimes you've got to do ridiculous things for cash.'

'You know it would've been a lot easier for you to just make coffee.'

'And make half the amount,' he replies in a joking voice. 'Anyway, tell me about your day. I miss you.'

'Yeah,' she sighs. 'I've actually got to go. Exam tomorrow.' Then, she hangs up.

## FAMILIAL REUNIONS

⚘

The next day, Lori decides to tackle another item on her list before heading to her night shift. She tips the box of miscellaneous items destined for Trade Me upside down, letting everything splay across the ground. The floor is dirty, she discovers, this close to the ground, despite mopping weekly. It has that thin layer of grime that can only be fixed by a new polish. She turns a faulty alarm clock on its side, then returns to the floor, running her index finger along a panel before shaking her head. Some matching measuring cups stare at her with mockery. Mockery crockery, she almost jokes, but instead uselessly cups her hand and yells, 'Jaaaa-aaaaaames, are you awake yet?' Sometimes she prefers to interact with his situation over dealing with her own problems. His life still feels salvageable.

'Jaaaaa-aaaaaames!'

'Uaaagh,' James groans. It's nearly midday, but he can't open his eyes.

The thing is, despite James's complete and utter rejection of everything, the reason is not as clear-cut as he'd like to admit. He is really just afraid. He thinks he doesn't deserve anything, that any step into another person's world is a step too far. Ever since he was a child, he was shy, and as he's grown older, has become increasingly reclusive. Oddly enough, it was once his visits to Daphne's that saw him performing at full force – zooming around the house pretending to be an aeroplane, drawing all manners of monsters in his notebook, asking if he could help Daphne with dinner, reading entire books into the night by torchlight. At home and school, though, he clammed up. Closed his shell. There were small steps taken after high school, a part-time job at the Fish and Chip store, registration at the local polytechnic, and a small stint living in shared accommodation with international students primarily from America, but these steps had only driven his negative self-image through the roof, and required him to take three steps back, gradually, over time, the first being a return to his mum's home, the second – dropping out from his digital creativity course, and the third, a soft firing from the chippie on the grounds of not enough hours.

James's room has become both a sanctuary and prison. Time slips by with little evidence due to his blackout curtains. Day and night are treated equally – plugged into sleep and the online world at odd intervals. And the reason he can't open his eyes is that he was up till three in the morning talking to someone online with the username lexicon-power333. She said her real name was Lexi. They talked about almost everything they could, including James's relationship status. I can be your girlfriend, lexicon-power333 typed, and a small dose of unfamiliar excitement ran through his bloodstream. But when he added her on Facebook, she declined his request.

'Jaaaaa-aaaaames.'

'WHAT!' he screams.

'I'm taking this junk to the Salvation Army, no point in trying to sell it.' Lori says this last part a little quieter, as though reasoning with herself. 'And we'll need to re-polish the floor sometime.' A pause, then: 'And by the time I come back, you'd better be out of your bedroom!'

Ryan has run out of things to do without revealing himself. He can't study for his exams during the day unless he hides in his bedroom, which is number one on the list of what not to do, under strict instruction from Lori.

'It's not that she'll figure us out,' she said, as though they hatched the plan together. 'It's just that it might disorient her, seeing new technology in the house, and we don't want to cause any unnecessary confusion. Plus, she needs the company. I want you to spend as much quality time with her as you possibly can.'

He stands in the hallway, wondering whether to walk to the living room where Daphne is or just go to his bedroom. It's not like Lori would ever find out, but what Amy said the other night has been bugging him. He tries to remember what he was like with his own grandmother but remembers only Werther's Originals, the feeling of the inside of his mouth after sachet packet juice, and some kind of fruit tree short enough that he could pick the fruit himself. Mandarins? Ryan was only seven when she passed away, and despite assuring Lori he was a loving grandson, he didn't know what he meant when he said it. Should he tell Daphne he loves her? Or was he meant to do things with love? Like what? Sit with her?

Ryan walks back to his bedroom, closes the door, and perches on the end of the bed. To appease some of his guilt, he decides to text Lori.

*Hi Lori, Ryan here. Just wanted to let you know everything is going well over here.*

A few minutes later, his phone begins to vibrate in his pocket. It's Lori calling.

'Hey Ryan,' she says happily. 'Just checking in. How's your day going?'

'It's going good, thanks,' he replies.

Lori has just left the Salvation Army and is walking back to her car. She's feeling dissatisfied with how little time it took to deposit the items. It was meant to take her hours – if only she'd stuck to the original plan of listing them online – and now feels as if, by choosing this alternative route, she has somehow cheated herself.

'How lovely,' she says. 'But what about you? How are you?'

'Good. No complaints here.' The sound of the landline ringing drills softly through the house and he wonders whether he should help Daphne answer it. Before he has the chance to decide, Lori chirps back in.

'Missing rugby? Been getting outside much?'

'Uhh, yeah. I'm missing rugby.' He pauses for a moment to consider what to say next. 'A little bit. Daphne and I might go for a walk this afternoon.'

'Oh!' she gushes. 'What a great idea.'

Ryan never put much thought into why Lori needed him when there was a Real James out there, somewhere. He assumed he might be overseas. Now, he gets the sense there's something more obscure at play – that perhaps Lori wants more than a stand-in grandson, but a new son, too.

'I'm about to hop in the car, Ryan. Okay if I call you back in a couple minutes?'

Minutes later, Lori takes her shoes off and slides into her slippers, closing the front door behind her. She can hear James's voice, and her heart leaps excitedly as she clocks he has, in fact, left his bedroom. It is all going to be okay, she thinks. Caitlin will be so pleased to know the plan is progressing. The future is only up from here. Lori pads down the hallway, pausing outside the kitchen so she can eavesdrop but not be seen. He must be talking on the phone, because she can't make out another voice.

'Just been working on some stuff,' he's saying.

Lori smiles to herself, raises her eyebrows to no one.

'Yeah, pretty busy.'

Some silence.

'Oh, that's nice. What's the weather like?'

'Yeah, it's been good here too.'

Lori swallows. She feels heat pulsing through her cheeks – the only person James could be talking to about the weather is her mother, his grandma. She steps into the living room. James, still in his bed clothes, emanating an odd stench, is standing by the home telephone.

'James, uh,' she lifts a finger into the air. 'Are you on the phone to Grandma?'

He nods and rolls his eyes.

She moves her hand across her neck. 'Hang up, now, please.'

James puts his hand over the phone. 'Are you for real?'

Lori motions for him to hand the phone over.

'Mum, are you there?' she says, pressing the phone to her ear with her shoulder while she motions for James to leave the room.

'Lori, is that you?' comes Daphne's voice. 'Where did James go?'

'He had to go,' she sputters. 'Lots of homework.'

Real James is looking up at her with confusion. Lori can feel her heart sinking. This is all so wrong. Now he's motioning for her to hand it back over. She can't, she won't.

'Lori,' Daphne repeats. 'Is there something you need to tell me?'

'What are you doing?' James cuts back in, snatching the phone from Lori, nicking a small chunk of his mother's skin in the process.

'Ow!' Lori whips her hand away. There's a crackle as James lifts the phone back to his ear, but all he can hear is the voice of Ryan saying, 'Hey, Grandma,' as he greets Daphne.

It takes a moment for James to confirm with himself that he doesn't have any cousins. 'What's going on?' he turns to Lori.

'I can explain,' Lori says quietly. 'Just hang up the phone, please.'

He pushes down on the END button, slowly – so slowly.

There's silence.

'Who's staying with Gran?'

'Let me explain,' Lori begins, her voice already unsteady. 'I've been so worried about her being all alone.' The words begin to run into one another, and the lines on her forehead begin to rise. 'And you never leave your room, and I'm worried you might be depressed, and I love you both so much, and I thought if I could buy some time…'

James scrunches up his face in confusion. 'But who was that, calling her Grandma?'

'That's Ryan.'

'Who's Ryan?'

'He's a student, from Dunedin.' And just like that, the tip of the secret is revealed. The rest of it comes trembling, shaking out of the shadows, until James feels like he is seeing his mother for the first time.

'Why is he calling her grandma?' he asks.

'It was only temporary, while we waited for you to leave your room,' Lori whispers.

'We? I don't get it, you're... what's he doing there?'

'He's there to fill in, just until you're ready...'

'Does Grandma think he's me?' James asks, the emphasis on each word displaced. When she doesn't reply, his sadness turns to rage. 'This is so fucked up,' he snaps. 'Who does that? Grandma has dementia, and you've come up with some freaky way to use it against us. That's... evil.'

Lori looks at him, punctured. 'I'm not,' she says. 'I'm just trying to be a good mother, and a good daughter.'

'Well, nice one,' he says flatly. 'You've seriously fucked up both.'

Lori chokes, tears streaming down her face. She turns to put the kettle on, hoping it might calm everything down. By the time she turns back to face James, he's left the kitchen. The sound of items being thrown around reverberates through the house. Then everything goes quiet. A zipper is pulled. A bag has been packed. Before the water boils, she hears the slam of the front door close behind him. At least he's out of the house, she sniffs. The hiss of the kettle gets louder and louder.

⁂

Ryan is sitting on his bed, feeling completely unsure of himself.

'Are you in here?' Daphne says from outside his door. He stands to let her in.

'Hey, Gran,' he says. 'Are you doing okay?'

She's clutching the landline in her hand and her eyes are studying his face, moving from his chin to each of his cheeks before finding his eyes. 'You're not James,' her voice shakes.

Ryan's taken aback. This was never part of the plan. 'No, it's me Gran,' he mumbles before piping up 'James, Jay-Jay, remember?'

'No, you're not,' she says, her voice rising. 'I don't know who you are.' She furrows her eyebrows. 'Get out of my house,' her voice picks up, 'or I'll call the police.' She lifts the telephone and begins to wave it in the air.

He packs his bags while Daphne watches him, muttering words of disappointment – 'My James would never do something like this,' and confusion – 'What kind of human thinks it's okay to impersonate family and love?' that sink into him like lead. His whole face is flushed red. All he wants to do is call Lori and tell her how fucked up this is. While he shoves his clothes into his sports bag, he plans out what he's going to say. I want compensation, he'll demand.

By the time he's out of the house, dragging his feet down the street, he's given up. He turns a corner and begins to walk towards the bus stop, the strap of his sports bag digging into his shoulder. No more Student Job Search, he tells himself. No more money chasing. Maybe he'll tell Amy she was right. Maybe he'll even apologise to the necessary parties. Maybe.

⁜

Meanwhile, James is stomping down the stairs to the front garden. It's the first time he's been outside in months. The sun hurts his eyes. The lime tree has new buds preparing to sprout. The crisp air knocks him back, as though chemically reacting with his odoured skin. When he steps through the gate, the street before him stretches out as an infinite row of wooden houses. He looks back up at his own home, at the drawn curtains in the window of his bedroom, gives it a small nod, and continues. Lori's neighbour, June, is standing in her garden, holding a garbage bag full of mown grass. She looks up at James – who from where she's standing – looks more monkey than human. His knotted hair is wired with energy, matted into greased tufts, and his clothes stick to his skin in odd places, like just above his right nipple, and against his waist, and look like they'd smell of compost.

'Afternoon, James,' she smiles apprehensively. 'Good day for it?'

He pauses for a moment, taken aback. He looks up at the sky, he looks down at his shoes. 'Great day for it,' he laughs manically. 'A really, really great day for it.' He turns and walks on, slapping his feet against the concrete path. The air still feels too crisp for him, but he begins to drink it back in deep gulps. There's the faintest smell of daffodils. He strides past trees, picket fences, and driveways. A breeze picks up and washes over him, and still, he stomps. He'll never go back. This is the new rebellion.

# TWO WOMEN, SWINGING

Annalise and Josie have been meeting in Central Park ever since Josie's daughter, Charlie, was old enough to run outdoors. It's a convenient meeting place for them, despite Josie's initial declaration during pregnancy that she would 'never become one of those Central Park moms.' The large slab of greenery, only a small walk from Josie's Harlem apartment and a short drive from the school Annalise sends her twin boys to, rarely goes more than a month without a visit from them. Sometimes they propose a different outing – a drink, or dinner – but Annalise always cancels. There is something about the park that keeps their incompatibilities at bay. She isn't sure if Josie feels the same way.

They always meet at the same spot, a small sleeve of rocks near a set of swings where they can stand and watch as their children either swing or climb. Annalise likes it because it isn't far from the exit path, and it's much quieter than the other play areas. Sometimes – much like the drinks and dinners – they plan to venture further in with plans of a picnic on the Great

Lawn or a turn on the commercial rowboats. But, just as excuses present themselves in time for Annalise to cancel their friend dates – weather, sore stomachs and parking limits always spare her from going beyond the bend they always turn into.

※

One dewy weekday afternoon, the two women are standing on the bank, with their arms crossed over their chests, watching their children climb a boulder that Annalise thinks looks particularly faker than the rest. She often thinks they look fake – something about the way the bedrock jilts out at certain angles with its painterly shades of grey. Sometimes, when Annalise is feeling particularly agitated, she comments on it.

'Are you sure the rocks are real?' she says.

'Yes, they're ancient,' Josie replies, and drags a red boot through the mulch, revealing dead grass. Josie's daughter, Charlie, is scratching moss from one of the rock's crevices. Annalise's twin boys are sitting at the highest point, legs crossed, performing a gentle battle with two sticks.

'I've been thinking,' Josie says, 'it might be time I get a boyfriend.'

'A boyfriend?' Annalise laughs. 'What happened to the last one?'

Back when the two of them were in college together, they had used the term 'boyfriend' to casually describe any male they'd slept with. Now, it is used a little joylessly to describe Josie's interactions with Uber drivers or coaches from the kids' sports teams. A boyfriend no longer needed to kiss, or compliment, or fuck – just exist. In Josie's world, between raising Charlie and working as a vet's assistant, everything is an affair. Annalise doesn't work and is still with the father of her children.

'You mean the one from the supermarket?' Josie asks. 'The tall one?'

'Yeah. Jerry?'

'Jack,' Josie exhales. 'I haven't seen him since I bumped into him in the meat section, and no cell phone number, so.'

'You're ridiculous,' Annalise chuckles.

Something about everything Josie does is ridiculous to Annalise. At this moment, she's trying to stop herself from commenting on the buglike glasses Josie's wearing. Annalise, on the other hand, is wearing every type of neutral shade she can. Her husband, Tim, often jokes that she is 'wholly beige', and she's never sure whether to take it as a compliment. Her toes are poking out from light brown sandals, legs wrapped tightly in cream cotton jeans, with a camel-coloured cashmere jersey hanging to the exact length it takes to cover her zipper.

'I am ridiculous,' Josie lets out a quick smile, sliding the glasses further up her nose. 'But really, this time I think I'm ready. For a partner-boyfriend. I've been thinking about going online.'

It's been a long time coming, this offhand admission. Annalise had sensed there was something beneath their conversations as they pushed the children on the swings. She could feel it in the way Josie spun their usual domestic comments into something requiring company. It was subtle, and Annalise couldn't put her finger on it at the time, but now it seems obvious. Josie is lonely. Annalise has never used a dating app. They came into practice long after her and Tim were married. She doesn't think it's wrong to use them – has even heard of great romances that begin with them. It's natural to seek love, but something about Josie's declaration makes Annalise feel uncomfortable. The worst part, Annalise thinks, is that she's not sure if Josie can even see the gaping hole between them behind those stupid, stupid glasses.

'Have you been thinking about this for a while?' Annalise asks.

'No, just here and there,' Josie replies, and returns to dragging her foot through the mulch.

Annalise can sense there is more Josie wants to say. She has often admired this ability in herself – to assess body language, to read the unspoken. She could have been a lawyer, or a manager of some kind, she thinks. Instead of a wardrobe of beige, she could have been waking up to power suits, dry-cleaned and pressed by somebody else, coffee on the go, high heels that clacked down a hallway of stone. Instead, it feels like she spends her days administrating order out of disorder. Wiping chins, soaking stains, and wrapping sandwiches in glad wrap like little gifts. She can't remember the last time she exercised her brain for something other than analysing other people.

Meanwhile, Josie continues to drag her foot, widening the circumference of the freed grass. Worms wriggle over one another. Up on the rock, the twin boys have laid down their battle sticks and have made their way to where Charlie is playing.

'Aren't you worried Charlie's getting her dress dirty?' Annalise says.

'It was already dirty,' replies Josie. 'And besides, white doesn't exist in our household anymore.'

An image of stacked, crisp, white linen appears in Annalise's head. The last time she had visited Josie's – when had it been?

– there were leaning towers of clothes stacked high on the couch, and a pile of odd socks on the dining table. There was no order to the chaos in Josie's house. Colours ran rampant, chores got sporadic attention, and there was always, always, something that Josie had forgotten. Keys were left at work, shopping lists went unwritten, and fines incurred their own fines.

'A bit of bleach would do.'

Instead of responding, Josie audibly inhales. 'Oh my god,' she gasps, then smacks a hand over her mouth.

'What?' Annalise replies automatically, then looks to where Josie is staring. 'Oh, eugh!'

Beneath them, on the outskirts of Josie's foot made clearing, is a dead baby bird on its side. Its feathers are rain-soaked, plastered back, revealing its tiny, feeble, body.

'He's so small,' Josie whispers.

'So small.'

The bird's eyes are closed, and its legs lay flat. The two women stand over it, moving their faces into expressions like clay: concern, disgust, sympathy, stoicism.

'What should we do?' says Josie, and crouches down to inspect the bird up close.

'It's dead,' Annalise says decidedly. 'There's no saving it.'

'I know that. But just because something's dead doesn't mean—'

There is a silence as they each wait for the other to speak. The sun is getting lower, and the leafless branches have begun latticing the light across their faces. Annalise turns her gaze back to the children, who are now sitting cross-legged in a triangular circle atop the rock, exchanging whispers. It seems inevitable, Annalise reflects, that the children will grow apart. There will be plenty of opportunities for their pathways to peel off from one another. Secondary school, new peers, diversified interests, the dimming of their imagination, and the consequent loss of playtime as bonding. Would their growing apart finally spell out the end of her and Josie's friendship? Or could it be that the children would become those long-term friends that have their origin stories in childhood? Leaving the two women bound together for life?

'We could have a funeral for it,' Josie says with satisfaction in her voice.

'Jos, it's a bird.'

'Why does that matter?' Josie stands back up and begins surveying the area around them as though looking for a shovel.

'It probably died days ago. Its own mother wouldn't have a funeral for it.'

'Elephants mourn,' Josie announces, picking up a stick and inspecting its pliability by bending it slightly.

Annalise snorts lightly. 'They do not.'

'They do, I saw it on television. They take particular interest in the bones.'

Somewhere, on a nearby street, there is the honk of an ambulance, and the faint jingle of horse hooves trotting along concrete with tourists in tow. Annalise rummages through her leather handbag and pulls out her cell phone. In the search bar, she types 'animals mourning'.

Josie abandons the stick and waits as Annalise moves her manicured index finger around the screen – scrolling and clicking through to other pages.

'Okay,' Annalise eventually sighs. 'You might be right—'

'Thank you.'

'—about some animals. Elephants return to where the dead lay for weeks.' There's a pause as Annalise scrolls to retrieve further facts. 'Dolphins and orcas carry their dead for days. Chimpanzee's groom their dead, which is strange.'

'We technically do the same,' replies Josie. 'At morgues.'

Annalise shrugs. 'There's nothing in here about birds, except for magpies, which are intelligent enough to bury their dead beneath a pile of twigs.'

Josie's dress, which reminds Annalise of a Christmas tree, billows in a small gust of wind. The two women had spent Christmas together four years earlier, the two of them and their children, just after Josie's husband Franco left her and when Tim was away for work. Annalise had missed Tim, especially when they had been unwrapping the presents. Once the kids were asleep, the two women played records and drank what was left of the wine. At some point past midnight, Josie put her head out the living room window and screamed, 'Fuck you!' into the night, without explanation. Annalise had mistaken the way the room drunkenly slowed to a pause as something more cinematic than it was and clambered across the furniture to join Josie. 'Fuck you all!' she'd yelled, her tight bun letting loose a few strands, and Josie had given her the biggest smile of the night.

Now, Josie bends down and begins to clear a small plot of land with her hands, raking leaves to the side. 'If magpies can do it, so can we,' she says.

Annalise shakes her head, and mutters abruptly, 'Don't be ridiculous, it's unhygienic.'

'Pfft, I'll use my gloves and wash them afterwards.'

Annalise feels all kinds of knots tightening inside of her. 'What happens if you find a dead squirrel?' she says. 'Would you bury that too?'

'Maybe.' Josie begins to dig a small hole, scooping mud with her hands.

'Everything's going to die one day,' Annalise continues. 'You can't say goodbye to it all.'

'I know, I know.' Josie presses her hands against the wall of the hole, solidifying its structure. Then, she pulls a glove over her right hand, picks the baby bird up by its middle, and gently places it inside. It takes three handfuls of dirt to conceal its figure. She stands, peels the glove off, and drops it down next to her bag.

'See, that wasn't so hard.' Josie brushes her hands on her thighs, shedding dirt. 'I just think,' she begins, then pauses to let out a fake yawn. 'With so much time alone, not that I'm alone when I'm with Charlie, but you know. Charlie's at school, and my other friends have moved upstate, and I only see you once in a blue moon. It can get really empty. Things like this,' she gestures towards the miniature burial site, her voice beginning to wobble, 'remind me of my own humanity. Otherwise, I'm going to harden. Become some batty old woman.'

Annalise nods. She understands. Even if it is through faulty translation, she understands. She feels it mainly when Tim is away for work. It is difficult to describe, she thinks, the exhaustion that comes from being an adult alone. She tries to imagine a world without Tim's companionship, too, and simply can't.

'Makes sense,' she says quietly. 'So, a partner-boyfriend? Not just a boyfriend-boyfriend?' she offers.

'I'm done with boyfriend-boyfriends,' Josie smiles sadly.'

Several shrieks ricochet around the park. 'Get off OF ME!' Charlie yells. The twins are not exactly on her, but appear to have fallen over, stumbling into her legs.

The two women begin to descend the bank, stepping over brambles and puddles while they make their way to the scene down below to perform their practised interventions.

'So, what does online mean? Like an app?' Annalise continues, watching her feet as they move over the wet leaves.

'Maybe, but that might be a bit young for me, don't you think? I was thinking more of those good old-fashioned websites. Matchmaking. No neologisms.'

Annalise pretends to take great care stepping over the first small crop of rocks. 'I'm sure it's fine,' she says.

Annalise and Josie reach the bottom of the crop of boulders and crane their necks towards the child-sized silhouettes atop the largest rock.

'Charlie, get down from there,' Josie says sternly, then turns to face Annalise. 'No, but seriously, it might be embarrassing. I barely even know how to text. Let alone create a profile.' She looks up again – the twins have abandoned their wooden sticks and scrambled out of sight.

'It can't be that hard.'

'But what if it doesn't work? And I ruin Charlie's view of me as an independent woman?'

Annalise winces at the phrase independent woman. She has always found the term to be self-congratulatory. 'Then you keep on keeping on,' she says.

'I'm tired of doing all the keeping on by myself,' her voice wobbles again on this last part, and Annalise wonders whether Josie is about to cry. Somewhere, over the rock, Annalise can hear her twins talking. While she puts an arm around Josie, she thinks about them. She thinks about the impression Charlie might be giving them of girls, or women – and the type they ought to spend their lives with. They do not have any other girl friends. The first, Annalise thinks, has to be the most influential. And Charlie is very much the daughter of her mother. Yet she is also somehow more – it took time for Josie to build the confidence, and in turn, has provided Charlie with it early on. Annalise still remembers the first day she met Josie, in an office at elementary school. Josie was in trouble for giving another boy her seat. Annalise had been called in to explain why she had written her name on the teacher's desk. They had both been shy, timid things, afraid of their own voices.

She takes her arm off Josie's back. They stay standing there, and Josie pulls out a used tissue to blow her nose with.

'Remember that guy Raphael? The postman?' Josie says, returning to her catalogue of men, looking for ways to stop herself from crying, and then: 'What are they doing?' she chokes, the final tear drying as she lifts her arm to point.

Up on the rock, the two twins have come back into view. Charlie is standing between them, holding their hands. There is something ritualistic about the sight. Charlie's dress could be mistaken, from down where the women are standing, as an angel's cloak.

'They look like they're in a cult,' Annalise gasps, shocked.

'What're you doing?' Josie yells, cupping her hands.

'We're getting married!' one of the twins screams back.

'Mum, come!'

Annalise and Josie move closer to the base, stretching their arms to take hold of the slabs closest to them, tucking their toes into nature-made footholds. Hand after hand, foot after foot, they climb. Josie reaches the top first, and upon lifting her hands from the rock to stand, says, 'That was harder than it looks!' She looks behind her and watches Annalise's head comes into view.

'I think you're all a little young to be getting married,' Annalise huffs, brushing her pants free of debris.

Charlie nods, hands still holding the twins. There is a smear of dried chocolate ice cream at the corner of her mouth. 'But marriage can be done more than once,' she says assuredly.

Annalise raises her eyebrows at Josie.

'What? It's true,' Josie shrugs.

'Yes, but it's sacred,' Annalise says. 'Sac-red,' Lucas repeats to his mother. 'Can't we make this sac-red?'

Annalise looks down at her sons, then over to Josie. She's reminded of her own wedding day, the symmetrical flower displays and the way Josie made sure her dress draped the right way across the floor. There were other bridesmaids – Linn and Bella – who Annalise spends more time with, and is closer to. Despite this, it was Josie who arrived the earliest, which was surprising given her track record of lateness. It was also Josie who stayed by Annalise's side as Linn and Bella left the make-up room to mingle with guests. Annalise insisted she wasn't nervous, and yet, whenever something started to agitate her – the heat, the shade of her lipstick, or how a strand of hair was falling – it was Josie who calmly and swiftly dealt with it.

'Okay,' Annalise says, giving Lucas's mop of hair a light ruffle. 'If you're sure.'

By strict instruction from Charlie, each of the women walks their children across the top of the boulder. On Annalise's second time, walking her second son, Charlie yells. 'Wait! Who am I marrying first?'

Annalise laughs, and warming to the feeling of her son's hands in her own, says, 'How about we start over again?'

'Yes,' Josie exclaims. 'Charlie, you stand with me. Annalise, you walk the boys down together, and then I—' she pauses to pinch two corners of her dress so she can curtsy, '—will be the celebrant.'

After a series of nods, Annalise returns to her end of the rock, hand in hand with each of her boys, and waits for the signal to go. Josie begins to play an imaginary trumpet, her eyes bulging and her face growing red. Charlie, by her side, seems almost shy as she watches her suitors walking to their altar of sticks and stones.

'Alright then, let's keep this brief, shall we?' Josie grins.

'Do you, Jack Henderson, take this woman,' she pauses to whisper to Annalise, who is standing still. 'How does it go again? To have and to hold?'

'To have and to hold, from this day forward, for better, for worse, for richer, for poorer, in sickness and in health, to love and to cherish, till death do us part,' replies Annalise, staring up at the sky.

'Right. Do you, Lucas Henderson, take this woman, Charlie Garcia, to be your wedded wife, to have and to hold, even when you're broke, sad, divorced,' Annalise raises her eyebrows in Josie's direction but she continues on, 'loaded, wifed up with another woman, with a new kid on the way, to love and to cherish, till death do you part?'

'Josie,' Annalise says.

'I do,' Lucas interjects.

Josie takes a large sip of air. 'And do you, Lucas Henderson, also take this woman, Charlie Garcia, to be your wedded wife, to have and to hold, so that you might leave her one day, till death do you part?'

'I do.'

'Charlie Garcia, do you take these fine men, Jack and Lucas Henderson, as your wedded husbands, to have and to hold all of their mistakes for eternity, till death do you part?'

'I do,' Charlie declares with affection.

🞀

Afterwards, once they're back down on the ground, they take

their newlywed children to the swings. Annalise imagines the hot bath she'll have when she gets home. She will probably have it hotter than usual.

'Why did you say those things?' she asks.

'It was stupid, I know,' Josie replies. 'Sorry.'

'Do you think Tim and I…?'

'No. God, no. You and Tim are a beacon of hope.'

'We're not perfect.'

'But close enough. Anyways, whoever thought of a three-person wedding?'

The two women laugh.

'That was strange,' Annalise says. 'Why did they do that?'

'I don't know. I suppose a lot of what I watch includes a marriage or divorce or relationship of some kind. Charlie often watches with me before bedtime.'

'The boys have started asking questions, too,' Annalise adds. 'It used to be, "Why are hippo's dangerous?" and, "What if there's a burglar?" Now it's all, "Where do you go when you die? and what's a soulmate?"'

Josie giggles. 'It's going to get worse,' she says. 'They're going to get older.'

'It might be nice. Less mess.'

'I don't mind the mess. I'm more worried about the hormones.'

The two women return once more to silence, looking to where their children are twisting the seats of their swings in a tight coil. Charlie is the first to release, and her swing begins to whip around in circles freely.

'Maybe you should message the postman,' says Annalise.

'Really?'

'Yeah, I mean, he seemed nice. Good sense of humour.'

'It's funny, hearing you say that. I feel I get to the point of committing to the search, and then find myself thinking the opposite. Like maybe I am better on my own.'

Annalise shifts her weight. 'Who needs men,' she jokes.

'Probably me,' Josie lets out a quick laugh.

'You're an independent woman, remember.' This time, Annalise doesn't wince. Then, she walks over to the swing set, giving her sons an extra push, before sitting down on a vacant one, letting her bottom fall over the side of the leather slips.

'Oh, now that looks fun,' Josie says, and walks over to the swing next to Annalise. They push off from the ground, and the world begins to rock. The two women sit there, swinging back and forth. From Annalise's view, the world is shaking. For Josie, jostling. But sometimes they feel what the other has, meeting somewhere in the middle, the way all swings must.

# DAVE

When they first met, he talked at length about Bertha Benz, the wife of Carl Benz and the engineer behind the first petrol powered car. Emmy had just arrived at her shift. Dave was sitting at a corner table in the outside area of the café, facing the street, and it was sunny, in that way where everything seemed brand new again. She assumed he must have noticed her parallel parking her car, the way he so confidently led with motor talk. She had come into a 1962 Benz by way of luck – bought cheap due to an absence of foot brakes, but with a friend bold enough to drive it across town to a mechanic, never creeping over ten kilometres an hour, and slamming on the hand brake whenever the green lights decided to flash orange, then red. Emmy enjoyed the car. With it, she found herself inhibiting a more mysterious version of herself.

'Bertha knew a good thing when she saw it,' Dave continued. 'Met Carl, saw what he was capable of, invested her own money, and BAM. Married, kids, cars!'

He was shorter than Emmy, which made her feel comfortable. His face was set with wrinkles in unusual places, like someone had pulled at the loose skin, and it had set that way. 'I'm Dave by the way,' he said.

'Hello Dave,' she replied. 'Bertha sounds pretty ahead of the times, for those days.'

Dave laughed and began to jiggle his knee. 'He was good, old Carl,' he continued. 'Smart in the engineering sense, but not much up here business-wise.' He tapped the side of his head, then laughed again, as though they had both heard the tap echo. 'It was Bertha who got him to actually make the damn car.'

꧁

Inside, Emmy fast-walked to the storage closet and lifted an apron with somebody else's notebook still in its pocket over her neck.

'Late again!' laughed Antoni the dishie when she walked through the reflective steel kitchen.

'Funny again!' Emmy laughed back. She put on a smile as she entered the floor. Emmy had only had the waitressing job for three weeks, being just a month and a half out of high school. The café served American diner food along with Mexican dishes – fried chicken and quesadillas and enchiladas and apple pie. The chairs that surrounded each table were mismatched and fraying at the seams. It was all part of the aesthetic, she had been told during her interview. They were not meant to be like other cafés; it was meant to be strange, like stepping into somebody's eclectic living room. The walls inside were

## DAVE

decorated like fridge doors, filled with pictures of people that had worked there in the past – much older than Emmy, bearded or tattooed, and always looking happy to be there. Sometimes, Emmy would look at the photographs up close, and imagine an older version of herself, smiling comfortably like they were.

Emmy dragged an already dirty cloth across one of the tables, cleared another, and collected coffees from Kelly the barista. She selected pieces of brownie that were still square with tongs, dolloped puffs of cream or pools of yoghurt onto their sides, and exchanged dirty plates and plates of food with the kitchen. On a trip back outside to deliver someone's latte, she paused to speak with Dave once more.

'So, how do you know so much about cars?' she said.

'Time,' he coughed. 'Lots and lots of time.'

Emmy guessed Dave's age was mid-seventies. She didn't catch many old people in town. They tended to live up in the hills, somewhere more affordable, or in retirement villages.

Dave took a pouch out of his pocket, popped a single filter between his lips, and started to roll a cigarette. 'You know, not many people around these ways talk to an old codger like me anymore,' he muffled. 'It's nice to meet a friendly face.'

Emmy smiled. It felt good to receive a compliment, even if it was from an old man. She was in the midst of another bout of hating life. She couldn't remember when it had begun. Was it when her boyfriend had broken up with her? Or when she'd withdrawn her university application to work at the café? She was quite resolute in this decision. As painful as the job was, it didn't inspire the same level of agony that the student advisor had. Emmy had been unusually honest, and told the advisor she hadn't a clue what job she was interested in. Together, in a too-small room, they'd moved through sleekly printed pamphlets on different subject areas. Somehow they'd arrived on Environmental Science, which didn't do anything to Emmy, who had half-expected to leave the meeting with some small realisation, a little passion she could hold tangibly in her hands, something to propel her forward into the life that she thought must be waiting for her, just around the corner.

⁂

It didn't take long for Dave to return, and with him, a small gold emblem called the Divya Mantra Sikh Khanda, a junkish piece of gold decor for Emmy to drill into the radiator grill of her car.

'For good luck,' Dave said, grinning. 'On the road.'

'Oh, thanks Dave,' she replied.

The cheap looking gift touched Emmy in a surprising way, and she put down the dirty dishes she'd been balancing, and took the emblem in her hands as though it were something holy.

'And Bertha,' he continued, as though no time had passed since their first encounter. 'She was determined that Carl's prototypes had the potential to become a car. A car!' he laughed, spreading his arms wide to acknowledge all the parked cars around them. 'If it weren't for her, Carl would've just kept drawing up his little ideas.' He pinched his thumb, index and middle fingers together as though holding a pen, then mimed a scribble across the table. 'Would've just kept drawing and drawing!' he laughed again.

Emmy laughed too. 'That's insane,' she said.

## DAVE

'She was sneaky too. One morning, when the prototype had finally been built, she woke their two sons at the crack of dawn to take the automobile for its very first road trip.' At this point he paused and began to pat himself down, looking for his pouch. 'Bertha didn't even tell Carl about her plan, knew he was going to be all antsy pantsy, just left him a note. Then quietly pushed the vehicle out of the house so he wouldn't wake up.' He found the pouch in his back pocket, and began to roll a cigarette. 'Do you smoke?' he asked, raising the pouch for her to take if she pleased.

Before Emmy had a chance to respond, a customer tapped her on the shoulder and asked if he could please have some napkins.

'Of course,' she said, and turned back to Dave. 'One moment,' she told him.

There weren't any napkins in the tray by the glasses of water, so Emmy went back to the kitchen, to where the chefs Santiago and Angel were having a lively argument about which one of them would get their driver's licence first.

'Who do you reckon?' said Angel. 'Me or Mr. No Car?'

Emmy bent down to retrieve a packet of napkins from beneath the sink, then stood back up. 'I'd have to see it to believe it,' she said, not entirely sure what she meant, but they laughed anyway.

'So, then what happened?' Emmy asked Dave after a series of other tasks required to wipe her responsibility slate clean – giving the customer his napkins, putting through an order for a family of eight, and then, realising she'd put through double of what they'd asked for, going back to the kitchen to tell Santiago.

'Well,' he smiled with his teeth. 'She took off! On a road that wasn't really a road.'

'Not a road?'

'Well, she turned it into a road. But there was no cleared route, no road markings.'

'Sheesh.'

'And there were hills that the car couldn't get up!' he began to jiggle his knee again. 'But good thing she took her sons,' he went on. 'Got them to get out and push.'

'They pushed a whole car up a hill?'

'Well, it was the beginning of a car. Imagine a big tricycle, with big back wheels and a wooden bench big enough for three people.'

'Gotcha.'

'And fuel was a whole other thing. Old Bertha could get ligroin or benzene from a chemist, which she did in some small German town, and just like that,' he slapped his hands together, and then started to jiggle both his knees, 'she created the world's first petrol station, completely by accident.'

'Wow,' said Emmy.

'Still there today.'

Emmy nodded to show she understood.

'And everything went wrong. The car broke down, but she fixed it. Used her hat pin to clear a blocked fuel line. Wrapped a garter round an ignition wire when it needed insulating.'

'Jesus.'

## DAVE

'Jesus indeed. Jesus had to be looking out for her. Some luck, that lady had.'

They continued on this way, Dave and Emmy, him giving her stories and titbits of information that she didn't ask for and her accepting them as though they were a neighbour's cat, visiting without an invite, but not particularly annoyed about it, either.

Eventually, after telling him about a weekend where her car had run out of gas going up a hill, and how she had walked down to the petrol station, too stoned to think straight, somehow deciding it was a good idea to fill her drink bottle up with gas at the station, walk it back up the hill, and squeeze it into the engine, he asked if he could have Emmy's number. She gave it to him, mildly aware that he wasn't just asking for it in case she ran into car issues and needed help, and not long after, he asked if she'd like to meet for lunch.

🜎

She wasn't scared when they first met outside of work. It was midday and they were meeting in the Starbucks of a food court attached to the main cinema in town. Emmy's friends told her it was creepy. Jamie, in particular, said it was super creepy, and that no seventy-something-year-old should be hanging out with a seventeen-year-old. They were sitting on the couch at Jamie's flat at the time, the cushions beneath them covered in stains and cheap fleece blankets. Emmy took offence. 'Can't two people of different genders and ages enjoy each other's company?'

'No,' Jamie assured. 'It's a well-known fact. There have been studies.'

'What studies?'

Jamie had smiled at Emmy in a patronising kind of way, and her eyes had darted over to their other friend, Jill, who had his lips around a bong, who also gave Emmy eyes that said he didn't believe a word she was saying. Emmy laughed. 'Seriously, guys,' she said. 'He's a lonely old man. When you're that age, you've got zero sex drive.'

⚘

At Starbucks, he told Emmy to order whatever she liked, and so she got a ham and cheese toastie and a caramel frappé. They sat opposite one another at the low couches near the window and he pedalled through all the different cars he'd owned in his lifetime, and then started to tell Emmy how he was going to buy a convertible soon, and he could take her for a drive, top down, if she'd like. The toastie was soft, limp, and too salty, but Emmy tried to eat it as politely as possible. When she set her cutlery down and took a sip of the frappé, she thought about how he had never mentioned a wife or children, and could be on his deathbed, in fact, dead within years, and what if a few years of friendship landed her even the smallest of inheritances? A car, or twenty thousand dollars, could change her otherwise aimless, pointless life. Emmy knew it was rude, but the idea excited her beyond anything else that year. Then he started telling her about how he was going to write a book, that tomorrow would be the first day of a very long writing journey, and she started nodding animatedly back at him at all the right moments.

## DAVE

🟊

Outside of work, Emmy still felt her life was going downhill. Her shifts finished at around 1:00am even though the café closed at 10:00pm. They had her cleaning for upwards of three hours, carrying the outdoor tables in, soaking the lids of the hot sauces in ice cream containers of hot water, doing stocktake, cleaning the pie freezer, and everything else, for she was the cheapest employee on payroll. Then, if she had the energy afterwards, she'd go and get stoned, or maybe drunk, or sometimes both. If it was the weekend, Emmy would shower at whoever's house her friends were congregating at, and definitely get drunk. When she had a day off, her and Jamie would just drive around, playing the same playlist over and over again, until they found somewhere they wanted to pull into – on a hill or by a beach, and turn the engine off so they could smoke a cigarette and look at whatever they'd chosen to look at. Jamie was also experiencing her first heartbreak, and it had brought them even closer as friends. They were different kinds of heartbreaks, but they inflicted the same level of hopeless yearning for said ex. The amount of time they spent rehashing what had been said or not said was unproductive, but it was all they seemed capable of doing. In between those misery moments, Emmy would receive texts from Dave. Useful titbits of information on cars, or recounts of his day, or sometimes just a simple 'how are you?' or 'are you working today?' Whenever Emmy opened her phone and saw a message from him, she was neither delighted nor peeved. She just saw them as a small arm outstretched into the void, asking for a handshake.

🟊

One afternoon, there was a massive windstorm while Emmy was working. She'd driven around for hours the night before with Jamie, stoned, feeling like they were going 100 kilometres an hour when really it was no more than twenty. Parked over by Shelly Bay, Emmy had experienced flashes into the future, and watched as all the adults in her life had reached down from the sky and stuck their arms right through her chest. It had been overwhelming, and her heart had palpitated at a worrying speed. The two of them had sat there in silence, breathing heavily, staring straight ahead through the front window of the car, until they'd finally gotten hungry enough to drive back to Jamie's flat and microwave packet pasta.

So, Emmy felt particularly spacy when the storm came in. They had to close all the doors to the outside area and bring the tables in early, which Emmy did with surprising ease. Barely anyone came in all day, just a cyclist needing a coffee, and eventually, Dave. He was in huge spirits, his body moving up and down as though he were jumping with his feet still planted on the ground.

'What are you so happy about?' Emmy asked.

'You got a break soon?' he bounced.

Emmy got her phone out of her apron pocket to check the time. 'I can break in twenty,' she said.

'I'll have a coffee while I wait.'

Emmy went behind the register and tapped his order into the machine. He walked over to one of the seats by the window.

While she waited for her break to begin, she went out back to the freezers where they kept the pies and got a head start on checking their best-by dates. It was freezing, and she could see her breath coming out in plumes of smoke, like she had something inside of her trying to make its way out.

She joined him at his table for her break. His coffee would have gone cold by that point, but he continued to sip at it while she made her way through a plate of French toast.

'Last night I had the craziest time,' he grinned.

'You have a night out on the town?'

'Not quite, but almost. Me and these girls had dinner. Met them on the street, Li and Becca. Li's a real feisty one, had heaps to say about her day. Becca's a bit more on the quiet side, but she's very beautiful.' He took another sip of his coffee. 'And well, we got talking, you know, and decided to go for dinner. My treat. Went to some place on the waterfront, and drank till we couldn't stop laughing.' At this, he leant back in his chair, looking positively smug with himself.

Emmy found herself feeling annoyed. 'Was it romantic?' she asked.

'No, friends only,' he laughed. 'I'm too old for that.'

'How old are they?'

'Gosh,' he looked out the window. The tree nearest them looked like it was straining to stay straight. 'Late twenties, early thirties. Hard to know.'

'That sounds nice,' Emmy said, and began to cut her banana into bite-sized pieces, placing one on top of a corner of the French toast.

'We should all go out some time,' he continued. 'Me, you, and the girls.'

After that, Emmy didn't want much to do with him, but he continued to visit, and she continued to serve him. One afternoon, he looked particularly glum, and she asked him what was wrong.

'Those girls,' he began. 'They've stopped replying to me.'

'You need something sweet?' she asked.

'Please,' he replied. 'Maybe some of that brownie, if you've got some.'

Emmy got him a slice and dolloped the cream on herself. 'On the house,' she said when she placed it down in front of him.

'Too good to me,' he smiled. 'What would I do without you?'

Emmy had, out of spite, spread her wings further than Dave. When Paulie from Lower Hutt came in, she made more of an effort to learn about his life. It turned out he worked in oil, and spent half of his years off-shore in the Arab Emirates. The woman with the bob, who Emmy learnt was called Michelle, owned two cocktail bars in the city. Emmy figured the more she talked to each of them, the more chance she had of coming away with something. She could be the lovely waitress they confided in, or the vulnerable girl they would one day want to give a leg up in the world.

Still, Dave was the main regular. He was the one whose company Emmy found herself genuinely enjoying. There was something in his nature, his smile, that made her feel comfortable. As though he were family.

They met a few more times at Starbucks before Dave suggested they go to his house. 'I really want to show you the draft of my book,' he said. 'But it's all scraps of paper.'

## DAVE

His house was nothing like Emmy expected it to be. One, it wasn't really a house, just a small flat on the ground floor of a shared building, and his bedroom was in the living room, separated by a bookcase lined with DVDs and cheap paperback books. His kitchen reminded her of the communal kind you find at camping sites, where kettles were made of white plastic, toasters had rust stains, and shelves were stacked with a variety of half-clean branded mugs. The only piece of art he had hanging was of a 1950s pin-up girl, and everything smelled of either cat fur or cigarette smoke.

When he went over to the kitchen to boil the kettle, he looked different to how she usually saw him. His hair no longer looked combed, but a little greasy, and his clothes had grown pills.

'Where do you park your convertible?' she asked, hovering in the doorway.

'Getting it next week,' Dave replied. 'Life's on the up.'

'Up and up.'

'Truly is. And next week, I start getting my superannuation payments.'

Emmy was surprised. 'Your first?' she enquired.

'Yeah, it's my birthday next week. Sixty-five. Whoopee,' he did a little jig and then bent over to pull a box of teabags out of the cupboard.

He started saying something about going out for dinner with the girls, they had gotten back in touch, and that Emmy was invited, if she'd like to come, but she was stuck on the revelation that he was only sixty-five. And, that he was broke enough to qualify for the benefit. Here he was, much poorer and much younger than she'd expected.

'Have a seat,' he said, gesturing to the bed.

Emmy looked at it apprehensively, assessing its cleanliness, before perching on its edge. She crossed her legs, then uncrossed them again. She could hear two men talking outside, loading boxes into a truck, saying something about tyre pressure.

'How long have you lived here?' she asked.

'Six months, maybe seven. Got stuff coming out my ears!' He waved his hands in all directions.

'Where'd you live before this?'

'In a van. Gotta say, it's nice being back in four walls. Piece of paradise. Milk?' he asked.

'No, thanks,' she said, shifting in her seat, twiddling her fingers together.

'Can't believe this is the first time I'm making you something,' Dave coughed. His lungs sounded full. 'You've been so good to me.' He carried the mug across the short stretch of floor and handed it to her.

'Thanks.'

He sat down on the armchair, which released small particles of dust that the sunlight caught. Emmy dwelled on the ex-boyfriend again. How was it, she thought, that even in moments like this, he was still on her mind?

Dave started rolling a cigarette. There was an ashtray at his feet. Footsteps came from the flat above, and there was the bark of a woman telling off her children. 'That's the thing,' he said. 'Too many people in this building,' he coughed again.

Emmy wasn't sure where she'd imagined Dave lived.

## DAVE

It hadn't been anything flash – no glass doors, or staircases. She supposed it had been something akin to the small brick house her Grandad had lived in. Details of the building were fuzzy, but accompanied by certain senses – radiator waves of warmth, the smell of roast potatoes, and knick-knacks in glass cabinets clean of dust. Looking around, she could not help but be repulsed by the way Dave lived. There was nothing homely about it. Furniture hid beneath piles of abandoned books, DVDs, and newspapers. An intellectual wasteland. Plates were left in odd places, atop piles of magazines, and the carpet looked thick with dust. The more Emmy looked around, the more she was repulsed. Yet in the same stroke, if she stopped taking in everything – the stained wallpaper, the leather belts, the congealed hand cream – and trained her gaze on Dave's face – she felt even more ill.

'Here,' Dave said, pulling ten or so A4 pages out of a notebook next to him. 'This is the scene where I think it's really getting good. The characters have really come alive. You know that's what they say, hey? That once you've put in enough writing time, the characters come alive, and all you have to do is follow them?'

Emmy nodded. She hadn't heard that, but it sounded convincing.

'I can't tell you how good it feels to be writing again,' he said.

Emmy tried to imagine where he spent his time writing. Was it in the same armchair he was sitting in now, or folded into the blankets of the bed beneath her? She imagined pieces of paper scraping against his forearm as he turned them, their thin sheets strong enough to shake flakes of dead skin loose. She tried to focus on what was in front of her. The pages came from an exercise book – they had the same faint blue lines she'd thought only schoolchildren used. It was handwritten in messy cursive loops.

It began with a man and a woman sitting on a bench near a lake. They were sharing a picnic, and the man, whose name was Max, was silent and sad. This was worrying Julia. So between mouthfuls of sandwich and sips of coffee from a flask, she asked him what was wrong, and when he still didn't answer, she said, 'Oh, Max. There is no need to be sad.'

Then, when Max still didn't reply, the writing went into Julia's stream of thought. She apparently thought Max wasn't getting treated fairly at work, that his ideas on how to better the business were being disregarded unfairly. Then, Julia began to feel a tingle in her vagina, aroused by the sheer intelligence of her boyfriend, and simultaneously angry that the world wasn't helping him, but it was okay, she would help him. Then Julia was standing up from the park bench, kneeling on the ground, and peering up into Max's sorrowful eyes, unbuckling his belt. His penis was soft and small, and again, this made Julia feel like he deserved so much more. She placed her mouth around the tip of his penis, then slowly brought it into her mouth, feeling it stiffen and grow. At first, she sucked very slowly, but then, feeling Max's hips thrust, she began to give him head so fast that it felt as though it were him fucking her in the mouth.

Emmy swallowed.

'Do you like it so far?' Dave said.

She blinked. Her head hurt, and her mouth was dry. She didn't know where to look, and so she continued to

## DAVE

stare at the pages, even though her vision had entirely disconnected and the words were no longer distinct – just small black and white etchings.

'Well?' he said.

She brought her eyes back into focus. 'It's quite sexual,' she said slowly. She could feel her cheeks growing red.

'But it's about so much more than sex,' Dave mused. 'It's about what's behind the sex.'

Emmy nodded. She pretended to look back through the pages, searching for something else to comment on. 'You're missing a punctuation mark here,' she said, then gently put the pages down on the bedspread as though they were fragile. Still, she did not get up.

Dave furrowed his eyebrows, studying her face.

Emmy could feel the panic rising in her. She needed to figure out a way to leave. She tried to appear calm, unaffected, then let out a nervous laugh.

'You don't like it,' he said matter-of-factly. 'I've made you uncomfortable.'

'No, no,' she replied quickly. 'Not uncomfortable. I've just never read anything so…' her voice trailed off, 'I've never read anything like it.'

He tilted his head, studying her. For a long moment, he said nothing. Then, he spoke.

'You're lying,' he announced slowly, then in quick succession, 'I thought we were on the same page. I thought you were smart enough to see what it's really about.'

'No, I see it,' she nodded. Her heart was pounding in her ears. 'Really, I do.'

'I'm no creep,' he replied, his voice rising, then his face went pale. He set his mug of tea down.

She was on her feet. She half-expected him to stand up too, and felt the adrenaline in her body preparing to run. 'I've got to go and help my friend,' she said quickly. 'I'm sorry to rush off.' She began making her way to the front door. Dave made no move to stand, just looked at her with accusatory eyes. 'I'm sorry to rush off like this,' she said again. 'But my friend.' She lifted the latch of the door open. As she stepped outside, a gust of wind blew in. The last thing she heard was Dave repeating himself, 'I'm no creep.' She slammed the door shut. She walked hurriedly down the driveway, past the men who were still unloading the truck. 'Oh my god, oh my god, oh my god,' she gasped to herself. She would need to quit her job, she decided, immediately. She kept walking until she was on the main road, then she started to run. The sky was too bright. The world was all there.

Five years later, on an awkward reunion walk with a different ex-boyfriend, Emmy and Dave cross paths once more. It is sunny, like that day they first met, and it is on a road bordering the park up the hill from the café, which still exists but is now owned by someone else and called something else. Emmy no longer lives locally. She is only visiting for the holidays.

When Dave notices her, a smile spreads across his face. 'You!' he beams, getting out of his car. 'It's you!'

## DAVE

'Oh my god,' Emmy says, turning to the ex-boyfriend, whose name is Marc.

'Who is that?' Marc says.

'It's this guy who used to be a regular at my old job.'

'He looks kind of odd.'

'Yeah,' she replies, looking over at Dave. 'Can you wait here?'

Marc nods, and Emmy walks over the slope of the hill until she's a metre or so from Dave's car. She recognises some of the items from his previous home – lampshades, magazines, and blankets matted with spikes, packed high in the back seat. They create a wall between the seats and the boot, which she realises has a small inflatable mattress in it.

'Hey,' she says.

'I can't believe it's you!' He stamps a foot and swings an arm cheerfully as if in America, on a rodeo.

Emmy lets him hug her, but she keeps some distance between their bodies as they embrace. A smell lingers on him – slightly musty, slightly salty. He looks much older, and had it been her first time meeting him, she would have guessed he'd be in his nineties. But, doing the maths in her head, she realises he will have only just entered his seventies.

'What are you doing here?' she asks. 'Is this your car?'

He grins again. 'Boy oh boy,' he exclaims again. 'This government, that government, each put me in my car to live,' he says, then pats out a tune on his knees. 'Sounds worse than it is, but this gal does me good.' He pats the trunk – the area that would be the car's arse.

Emmy doesn't know what she feels. It isn't pity, but it also isn't apathy. It is just a small flicker of thought that this is how the pieces of the world fell.

'And you?' he asks. 'You back at the café?'

'Just catching up with an old friend,' she gestures in the direction of Marc, who has pulled out his phone and is typing something out.

'Good looking fella,' Dave says.

'Guess so.'

'You two,' he flicks an index finger between them.

'No,' Emmy smiles. 'We used to date.'

'Tell me about your life, sweetie. It's been so long.'

She grimaces slightly, then retrieves her small talk. 'I wound up going to university after all,' she says. 'Got a degree, been living up North, painting.' She hates the way it sounds as though she's gotten her life together using all the usual methods – study, self-expression, a new setting – but it's true. She feels she has finally reached a point of quantifiable confidence.

'You always were a smart cookie,' he says.

'Like Bertha,' Emmy jokes.

A small look of confusion crosses Dave's face. 'Bertha?' he replies. 'Who's Bertha?'

Above them, trees creak. The direction of the wind is changing and will change again. A bird glides over them, then switches paths.

# PAINTING WORK

And then Albert picked up his paint bucket – he'd had enough of the man's positivity. And where had he come from? New faces were not a part of life in their town! Albert had lived here his whole life, and his introductions to its segments had come in simple sweeps. Family had been first – an ordinary sort of household: mother and father, reliable work horses, and two equally cheeky sisters that Albert used to share baths with each evening. Then there was school, with its students and the teacher, Mr Fowler. Of particular importance from the school era was the emergence of Albert's now best friend, Carlos, and his soon to be wife, Janine. Reaching cognisance, Albert had come to know the other townspeople too – the baker, banker, train driver, barber, mechanic, shopkeepers, and tavern staff. Then, reaching the ripe age of sixteen, Albert had taken on painting jobs along with anybody else from their year group that did not take after their baker, banker, train driver, barber, mechanic, shopkeeper, tavern staff parents (Carlos: painter, Janine: painter). Which had led him to his final round of introductions, to the people that lived in the Bays, where they spent their days painting. None since then, none to be had. Eight years and counting.

So what, Albert thought, had possessed this man to turn up to this shift today, and begin asking questions like, 'How is your day going?'

'My day is going just fine,' Albert had replied, before, as stated previously, picking up his paint bucket and moving out of hearing range.

Taking up station at a row of rose bushes still missing its petals, Albert sighed. He picked up his Sprucer Agent and the fallen petal nearest to him. Sprayed the Sprucer, and watched as the thin plate of the dead petal loosened its crinkle, spreading itself out healthy once more. Once all the leaves had been Spruced, Albert put them into an empty bucket before taking them over to the painting table, laying them out, and taking up a brush. Despite not being one for taking on extra work, Albert still possessed a level of care in his practice. He was often complimented on his knack for shading more than, say, his jokes, or his physique, or anything else pertaining to his state of being. So he took his time with this stage, moving between brushes of various sizes as he smoothed the gradient on each petal from Aureolin Yellow to Orange Peel to eventually, at each tip, a thin line of Amaranth Red.

'That looks lovely,' the happy man said, having walked over to the station. Albert looked up at him blankly and assessed what was in front of him. Older than him, sixties? Wonky teeth, thinning hair, but oh so smiley. Albert knew he should reply with a simple thank you, but did not have the energy to do so, and instead looked away. Picked up the Dry Heat Torch, without saying a word, and began to move it through the air above the petals, till, finally, the man gave up watching and walked back to the bush he had been spraying green.

⁂

After work, Albert left Kensington's without waiting for Carlos. He felt like being alone, as he often did. He walked along the wide lanes with careful steps, stopping all together when he felt like looking at one of the many mansions of the Bays. Albert often found himself entranced by the varieties of grandeur the Bays possessed – the way some homes had archways where others had wraparound porches, how each gate had its own unique pattern, and the edging cornices, their own style. It took him about ten minutes to reach the train station, where he boarded and sat in his usual window seat. The train remained still as more painters slowly shuffled on and sat in their own silences. Eventually it pattered to life, wobbling out of the station, passing by homes with gardens so large they may as well be called paddocks, filled with delicately designed and painted shrubbery, until the train began to pick up speed, and soon they were bolting for the river. At first the channel of water remained blue, but as they advanced across the bridge, it shifted from the desired shade of Azure and faded to Cyan, then to a Milky Baby Blue, until eventually it was grey, with unsynchronised patches of blue holding onto the surface. The dye they used for the river did this eventually – clumped into circles and drifted further than it was meant to. Soon, there weren't any patches for Albert to look at either, just a grey expanse of water, until they reached land again, and they passed by mounds of grey dirt, slowly entering the outskirts of Stokestown. Everything was grey in Stokestown – the sky, the stacked buildings, the ground. That was just how life was.

🔻

Marina, having watched the painters depart her uncle's house from her private balcony, decided it was time to go outside. She had recently lost the knack of receiving energy from company or distraction, hence her recent move to Uncle Kensington's. Kensington had, despite their wider family tree's tradition of being 'all-knowing', remained a private man amidst the throng, and so she had taken it upon herself to visit him for some alone time. Even at dinner, sitting across from her uncle, the staff setting down each course with the appropriate cutlery, Marina felt she was alone – largely because nobody spoke.

She took off her slippers, tied up her boots, made her way downstairs, and stepped foot outside. The air still smelt ever so faintly of paint fumes, but that was not unusual. As she meandered among the rose bushes, admiring the paint job of each petal, she thought about the family psychiatrist, Dr Barkley. In particular, she thought about the way he remained silent for long pauses after her answers, as if waiting for her to elaborate, before asking the next question. It simultaneously unnerved and calmed her. She was glad to know Dr Barkley wasn't being flippant with his speech, but she was also unaccustomed to it, more familiar with the style of speech she likened to yabbering – wherein her Mother and Father and siblings and aunts and uncles (save for Kensington) just talked and talked and talked, for there couldn't be anything worse than silence, could there? She thought also about Dr Barkley's observations on her situation, on where she could go from here. 'A common realisation for people in your position is that they lack purpose. Because one does not need to work out of necessity, one becomes in dire need of hobbies, but sometimes, hobbies are not enough for certain temperaments. Then there's parenting, which should you have children, will provide a wonderful source of fulfilment. Even then, I will, forgive me, be somewhat blunt, you will not be as accustomed to the demand it puts on the self, but again, because of your position, you will have help. Maids, nannies, and so on. For now, though, with your not being pregnant, or in love, I would encourage you to think about the hobbies you have tried. You mentioned art, and journaling. Those are both good. But think, is there a branch within each of these that perhaps you could hone in on? Are you more inclined to paint portraits, for example? Or write poetry? The more time you give something specific, the more specific its returns will be.'

The whole conversation had made Marina feel useless, because in a way, she reasoned with herself, she was. She was not a cruel person, nor did she take advantage of people. For the most part, she looked upon people kindly, but nothing she had ever done was particularly kind, save for the absence of doing unkind things. But was the absence of action an action? She didn't think so. She kicked her boot into the green grass, and kept kicking, until the green sprouts gave way to grey mud. 'Dammit, okay,' she said to herself, before pushing her shoe into the grass on either side of the hole, so that it closed up once more.

⁂

Having gotten off at his stop, Albert began his walk home, listening to the humdrum tide of the day slow after the rush of people clocking off. There was the faint sound of children playing outside, but no children to be seen, just the tall chain-link fencing wrapped around the roof of the school, and someone whipping a bed sheet through the smog, and a dog barking at nothing. Then, on the corner of Billah and Charles Street, Albert was confronted by a group of non-painters crowding around something he couldn't see. Mrs McCofty, the local baker, was standing at the back of the crowd, and so Albert gently tapped her on one of her hunched shoulders and asked, 'What's going on here?'

'Gas leak,' she replied.

Sure enough, steaming out from a metal grate in the sidewalk, was a thin orange mist. It curled in and then ballooned upwards, like it was dancing, before the grey air of the town met it, diffused it, and the colour evaporated. This was a semi-regular occurrence – every two or three weeks something started leaking colourful chemicals in Stokestown. Yet every time, it was as though the phenomena had never occurred, especially for those whose job did not take them to the Bays, and everyone's eyes bulged at the colourful sight.

Albert stood there, fixated, imagining the orange gas as someone's voice, travelling through the underground pipes all the way from the Bays to Stokestown. He thought, maybe this gas is a sign from the Gods. Then he looked past the heads of people still mesmerised by the gas leak, spied the happy man strolling towards him with a smile on his face, and began to walk briskly away, towards home.

## PAINTING WORK

At dinner, Marina and Kensington sat in the same chairs they had been sitting in for the past week, only this time, Kensington asked her a question.

'How are you enjoying your stay?' he said. Then, looking somewhat embarrassed, added, 'I don't mean to pry. It's just your mother called, and she asked.'

'Oh, that's quite alright,' Marina replied. 'You can tell her I'm having a good time.'

He nodded. Kensington was a gentle man. He had not always lived such a private life, having grown up with Marina's mother as a sister, along with their four other siblings. But the older he'd become, the more he had come to believe that retreating into himself was the most suitable way for him to get by. Parties, sports, politics and dinners all gave him unpredictable surges of anxiety, and though he used to gamble with it in his younger years, had learnt some uncomfortable lessons through it and decided they were no longer worth the risk.

Marina being in his house did not stir that fear in him, although he had found it somewhat strange that she had chosen to stay with him, given that they had never been close, and that when he had observed her at family events, she had always seemed remarkably social. The Marina in front of him now looked quite different – in her plain dress with her hair let free, and so awfully sad.

After the dishes had been cleared, Marina excused herself and went outside once more. She had never been one for wandering, so to speak. The act of seeing where her legs took her was an entirely new experience. Normally, going outdoors was for horse riding, or playing tennis, or admiring the newly painted nature. It had once been one of Marina's favourite pastimes, walking alongside her father through the tulip garden, inspecting the shade combinations the painters had come up with that season, then over to the orchard, where they stared calmly at the bright green leaves. But her recent wanderings did not belong to the same category – of observing the decorative landscape – but to something else entirely unnameable, as though she were no longer a person, but just a silhouette, or the shadow of something that had already walked past.

This time, she found herself down at the river, a mile or so west of Kensington's, and sitting down on the round solid stones. After several minutes of not noticing a thing, it wasn't the freshly dyed water that took her mind by the hand, but the thin line of grey on the horizon. The sky above her was grey, as it had been ever since she was born, but this was different, because this grey belonged to land. She blinked. She had never seen anything like it before, not from her or anyone else's home along the river, nor had anyone spoken of such a thing existing. Had it only just emerged, or had she simply never looked long enough? She stared a while longer, with her arms wrapped around her knees, until the line of grey land began to merge with the sky above, and she wondered whether it was just a trick her eyes were playing on her. Satisfied with this explanation, Marina prepared to look away, to continue walking, the route now entering the second half, in which it was time to return home. But just as Marina was getting ready to stand, a crane came into vision, exiting from a cloud above. It was an animal Marina had never encountered, and she found herself enamoured, even if just for a moment, as it glided with its wings outstretched, barely moving during its descent. Then at the very last moment before landing, it began to beat its wings in a flurry.

⁂

The next day, Albert woke in the basement room he shared with Carlos. The room was a mess, their two single beds rising out of a sea of strewn work clothes. Everything smelt like mud or paint fumes or the soft tang of armpit sweat. He went to the bathroom, kicked a wet puddle of towels into the corner, then took a shower.

Afterwards, the two friends stood at either end of their single beds and pulled paint-splattered overalls over their shoulders. They walked up the wonky stairs into the living room, both squinting their eyes at the grey natural light coming in through the kitchen window. The building was a shared house for painters – between ten and twenty people, depending on the number of people sharing rooms. It seemed most had already left for the train, because only Janine was in the kitchen, drinking back the dregs of a coffee.

'You coming with?' Carlos asked, and wandered over to give her a kiss on the cheek.

'A-huh,' Janine replied, and put her cup in the big tin sink.

Albert opened the front door and the three of them filed out.

'We're going to be late,' Janine announced, and so they began to skip their feet quickly down the concrete steps till they reached the road.

Upon boarding the train, Carlos and Janine sat on the only bench remaining, leaving the last free seat at the rear end of the carriage. It wasn't until Albert had walked down the aisle that he realised the free seat was next to the happy man, and sat down, despite his preference to remain standing, had it not come across as rude.

'Morning,' the man said.

'Morning,' Albert replied.

The man grinned, then shook his head. 'I know you must get it all the time,' he began, 'but your shading is magnificent.'

Albert looked out the window as the grey homes began to thin and the train yard came into view. 'Thank you,' he replied.

'Such care in the transitions, and in so little surface area, and on every single petal.'

'Thank you,' Albert repeated. From the front of the carriage, he could make out Carlos's voice and a laugh from Janine.

'Do you know what we'll be doing today?' the man continued.

Albert shrugged. 'Never know till we get there.'

---

Marina partially woke up, and finding herself with nothing to wake up for, retreated into a dream. Hours passed, until her body refused to sleep any further. When she drew back the curtains, she saw ten or so painters seated atop ladders, glueing leaves to the basswood trees, which meant it was past breakfast time, for they were well into their work, and she hadn't a clue what to do with herself. A thought suggested she go outside, but that was silly. So she took up a book, still in her pyjamas, and began to read lazily. Every few minutes she repositioned herself, unable to get comfortable. She tried reading under the blankets, lying down, then on top of them, then sitting up. Nothing on the pages drew her in, and the thought of going outside returned to her. Marina sighed, stood up, and walked back over to the window, leaning her hands on its ledge. The sky was even greyer than usual, and five painters down below had congregated over by the materials shed, discussing something, pointing at various buckets before placing their hands on their hips. The sound of someone playing piano, probably Kensington, began to slowly make its way through the house. On one particularly soft note, the crane reappeared down at the river edge, and Marina watched as it padded along the shore, and took it as a sign. She took her pyjamas off and tossed them on the floor, pulled a dress over her head and stuffed her feet into boots.

It was the first time she'd set foot outdoors when the painters were still working, and she walked through the garden slowly, taking in each of their faces. They were clearly worn down, but seemed almost content with their work, or at least too busy with the tasks at hand to become melancholic. Where Albert was bent over, spraying a rose bush with Primer, Marina paused. There was something odd about the way he was talking. Firstly, there was no one near him, and so it seemed he was talking to himself. Secondly, he took a great deal of time listening to, or ignoring, whoever it was he thought he was in the company of. Moving between looking at the air to his right, where somebody could have been crouched down next to him, and turning back to the bush as though no one was there, occasionally muttering under his breath. Marina couldn't make out what Albert was saying. She thought about getting closer, finding herself quite intrigued with whatever was unfolding in front of her, but then a breeze picked up and blew hair over her face. When she cleared it, tucking it behind her ears, she found herself facing the direction of the river. Remembering the crane, she started to walk.

🔺

Albert was glad not to be painting petals, for it meant the happy man couldn't badger him with incessant questions about his technique. When the man had sidled up to Albert earlier, when he was Priming, he'd humoured him with a little conversation. They mainly talked about Kensington. The happy man wanted to know how long Albert had been working on the property. Once two or three questions had been answered, he excused himself and walked over to where Carlos and Janine were preparing a large barrel of green paint, adding in Cadmium Yellow and Royal Blue until the required Spring shade of Emerald Green was reached.

'Can't catch a break,' Albert said, nodding his head in the direction of where the happy man stood.

'From who?' replied Janine, standing up straight.

'The new guy.'

'There ain't no new people,' Carlos said, digging a mixing stick into the barrel.

## PAINTING WORK

'Are you serious?' Albert laughed. 'You can't miss him, he's outrageously happy and won't leave me alone.'

Janine shrugged. 'Sorry, Al, think we'd know if we had a new person in our midst.'

Carlos started to stir the paints, then he paused. 'Would you mind taking over, Al? Janine and I haven't had lunch.'

Albert hadn't had lunch either, but he nodded, perplexed by his friends' inattention. He walked over to the materials shed and retrieved a Shade Reader, then dipped it into the barrel. A little more Cadmium was required to reach Emerald, and so he measured out a cup and poured it in. Satisfied with its reading, he gave the barrel five more stirs, then pulled the mixing stick out. He screwed the hose into the barrel, attached the Grass Filter before clicking it on, and walked across the lawn in a series of horizontal lines, watching as the aged job became gradually new again. He enjoyed about ten minutes of this before the man reappeared, and Albert let out an audible sigh, before switching the hose off.

'Yes?' Albert said.

'Sorry to bother,' the man replied. 'I know I'm pestering, but would you mind if we swap jobs? I'm useless at painting petals. You're very good at it.'

'Only way to get good is to practise,' said Albert, and switched the hose back on. It let out a whirring noise, not quite loud enough to block the happy man's second attempt.

'It's just, well, hmm.' It was the first time Albert had seen the man look something other than chirpy – a little confused, perhaps. 'Well, you see,' he mumbled. 'I'm colour blind.'

Albert switched the hose off once more. 'Colour blind?' he said.

'Yeah. The Achromatopsia kind – just black and white. So, you know, useless at all that stuff,' he said, waving his hand in the general direction of the petal station. 'I can wash and prime and glue, but when it comes to actual painting, well, I'm better suited to block colours. Like this here green. See, green is a dependable colour for me. Leaves are always green, so are bushes, and the grass – petals could be anything.'

Albert found himself with that feeling – where one knows they are meant to be sorry, but cannot access it. 'So, everything's grey?' he asked.

'More or less.'

'This whole garden?'

'Yeah. Some things are solid black, others are white. But mostly grey. I can still see shading; I wasn't lying with my compliments.'

Albert nodded.

'And I have seen colour,' the man added matter-of-factly. 'So don't feel too sorry for me.'

'When you were younger?'

'No, there's a place I can go,' he waved his hand around, 'to feel it.'

'Oh,' said Albert, and wanted to disregard the man once more.

'I can show you,' he said excitedly. 'If you'd like.'

'In the Bays?'

'No, not the Bays.'

'Where, then?' Albert replied with a light scoff.

'Hard to explain,' the man said. 'It would be a matter of trusting me.'

Albert began to formulate all the reasons he could not join the man and be shown. Then, his thoughts strung themselves into a long list of all the other times he had said no to people's friendly offers – Janine offering him a hug, or Carlos, a listening ear. And it wasn't that he'd regretted those times, he had been very steadfast in his no thank-yous, but the fact that he was all of a sudden acknowledging them, that made him think it could be okay to say yes, just this once.

🜲

Down at the river, Marina edged herself closer to the crane. From metres away, its legs looked like branches. With each step it took, its head darted forwards, with its long beak pecking at the air. It seemed to know she was there, the way it paused every so often and turned to look back at her, as though checking she was still following. Marina instinctively lowered her legs to make herself not seem too tall, or predatory, not that the crane seemed frightened. Together they moved like this, along the shore, until the crane stopped moving altogether, turned to look Marina directly in her eyes, and let out a low gargling call. Marina stood up straight. It did not sound like a warning, nor did it sound angry. Again, the crane gurgled, as though talking to her. Then it flapped only its right wing, and turned to walk on, only this time, much faster, but not at all like it was running away. Marina followed. Together, they made their way along the river edge. They passed by the front yards of the many homes of the Bays, the crane taking care as it crossed fallen logs or the piers protruding out from gardens and into the water. On they walked, the spaces between each home becoming larger and larger, until there was no sign of residents at all, just bush on the left, ashen and undyed, and a river on the right, which was steadily losing its blue.

Once their shift was finished, Albert wandered over to the front gate of Kensington's estate. He had, after many back-and-forth thoughts about whether it was smart to take the man up on his offer, decided it was okay, because it was a one-off. There was also a burgeoning curiosity in the man and his colour-blind condition. Something about the endeavour felt more akin to research than to socialising. His hypothesis being that the man could experience colour if it was of the intense kind, like if the saturation was knocked up to the nth degree, and only then could it break through his vision and appear as a pastel sort of shade. But then, Albert had reasoned while painting the petals he'd agreed to shade, the man had said the colour did not reside in the Bays. And the Bays were the only location for colour, save if you were lucky to spy a gas leak in Stokestown. Which made Albert think, was the man just confused about the border between the Bays and Stokestown? But how could one get confused about such a thing, when they were kept so separate?

Albert only had to wait a few minutes at the gate before the happy man arrived.

'You're here!' he said.

'I'm here,' Albert confirmed. 'Where we going?'

'We'll train over the bridge first. Then walk from there.'

Strange, Albert thought, and began to walk in the direction of the station without uttering a response.

'Thanks for swapping with me, by the way,' the happy man said. 'Made my afternoon a whole lot easier.'

'No problem,' replied Albert. 'Now, this colour, you sure we're heading the right way?'

'Yeah. It's always somewhere different. But the direction is always the same.'

🜲

At a certain point, the crane picked up and began to fly. The river was completely grey now, and the bush had gradually thinned so that as the crane turned a corner, Marina could still make out its wings, beating through the air. She walked quickly after it, trying to catch up, over stones and sticks, turning the same corner just in time to see it fly into a grey fog. As she went after it, everything else fell away. There were no longer signs of vegetation, nor water. Marina took a step forward, bewildered. The expanse in front of her went on forever. A grey stretch of land with silver, white, still air. It was like stepping into nothing, and still she went further, walking through the grey, looking for the crane, until she was running, running as though her life depended on it. It was nothing like runs she had taken in the past, where siblings were trying to catch her, or she was trying to come in first place, or Dr Barkley was encouraging her to move her body. It was completely freeing. Her legs dashed across the land without pause. She did not tire. The thing she liked most – how nothing around her changed. She could run and run and the surroundings around her remained the same. Life lifted her up and said, hello. You are Marina and you are running through nothing.

Albert, having followed the man onto the train and through the streets of Stokestown, taking lefts and rights that led him past all the ordinary sights – the bakery, the tavern, and so on – found himself reaching a road on the outskirts that he had never once in his life ventured past. And it was not that they had never been told to go further, but simply that the question had never been raised about what was beyond. The arrow had, quite simply, always pointed in the direction of the Bays. Albert watched the back of the happy man while the question of what was beyond unfolded within him. Struck by the incalculability of it all, Albert paused to consider whether to turn back. Then, as if his legs were one step ahead of his mind, he began to instinctually walk again, following the man, who now possessed some tug on his heart, without asking any questions. Together, they silently said goodbye to the final familiar landmark of the town, Mr Fowler's home, and it was then that Albert realised he had never asked the man for his name. It crossed his mind to pose the question, but something about it struck him as futile. They had, he thought, been walking in such complete silence for so long, that it seemed almost wrong to break it now. There was a pact of some sort, an unspoken agreement to reach their destination before words were exchanged. So on they walked, and as time passed Albert began to look around him, so that the man was no longer the central focus, but a guide. Unfamiliar buildings emerged, and soon Albert realised that they were moving through what must be another kind of town. Not dissimilar from Stokestown with its greyness, but different all the same. A slight shift in the pattern of the brickwork, and people in painting overalls that he did not recognise, making their way to their own version of the train station, to their own version of the Bays. Still, they walked on, and they ventured into new towns, with other delicate changes – a town with homes made from stone, and another with tin, and another with flax roofs – each one anchored to the existence of a shimmering line of mansions. It was, at times, overwhelming for Albert. They had been walking for many hours. As they began to depart another town, the signs of habitation receding, Albert committed to the notion that he would break his silence soon. He decided he would ask the happy man all sorts of questions – for his name, for an explanation, and then an explanation for that explanation. On the edge of the town, the man turned a corner, and when Albert turned that same corner, he could no longer locate him. He looked around him frantically, peering around the corners of the building. Ahead was empty, and so Albert ran back to the centre of the town and began approaching people on the street, exclaiming 'have you seen a happy man? You! Have you seen a happy man?' to which they all looked confused by the sight of him, let alone the question he was asking. The man had vanished into thin air. Albert looked down the road the way they had come, figuring it was time to turn back, that it was over, whatever this was. But, with that same instinctual need, and an understanding that the man had meant him to go on, he did not. Instead, he turned to face forward, and pressed on. Just as each town had receded into emptiness, this one did too. But after a while of walking, signs of another town did not arrive. Instead, Albert was surrounded by nothing. It was not like the usual grey he was accustomed to, for it was empty. Just a long stretch of time in every direction. He walked on, and with each step, he began to feel his heart gradually turning itself inside out. These were not emotions he understood, and so he looked ahead of him, hoping for the man to re-emerge. He turned to look back, only to discover that he had ventured so far into the nothing that he had lost sight of the previous town, and in doing so, had lost all sense of direction.

It felt to Marina as if she could have been running for hours, days, months, years. Nothing in her body told her to slow down, or stop. She could have continued for exactly that – hours, days, months, years – if it had not been for the small hint of something glowing in the distance, and then she stopped, slowing to a walk, finding herself quite afraid. With each step she took, it grew, and suddenly she found herself running once more, running and running, and the glow grew, and she saw a haze of colours, red and blue and green, and still it grew, but still she ran, and she was finally no longer afraid, until she was sure she couldn't stop, and then she was inside the blitzed cloud of colour.

## PAINTING WORK

Albert walked on until the same mysterious glow entered the no-scape, to which he furrowed his eyebrows. 'Strange,' he said aloud to himself, as though wanting someone to acknowledge and reply. As he got closer, the glow grew, and with it, its colours. At first, Albert could only spy its centre – an orb of yellow dashed with orange, but as the distance between himself and the glow closed, he was able to make out an uneven frame of green around the yellow, which with further steps, moved into a light blue. It was not an ordinary shape, either. It did not move out in circular rims, but rather, as though someone had painted it – beginning small at the top, then lurching wider to the right, and wider, till it turned in on itself, multidimensionally, and lurched back up. Still, Albert walked further up to it, entirely unafraid for what he felt was the first time in his life, watching as it hovered in the air, the blue moving into purple, until finally, particles of pink hovered around its edge, before fading into the air. Whether it was fractured light or another chemical failure, Albert wasn't so sure, but something about it felt entirely devoid of explanation. He lifted his hand in the air once he was below it, and slowly, began to move through it.

# DELIVERYWOMAN

In the corner of the pharmacy where I work, near the rows of postcards, there are yellowed photographs of the way Lambton Quay used to look. Of the four of them that are tacked to the wall, two are black-and-white ancient from before my time, filled with trams and top hats and flags billowing in the wind. The other two are more recent. In the first of these, you can make out a girl running past a row of taxis towards another girl, both of them the age I would have been when the picture was taken. In the next one, a car has pulled up in front of the taxis, and the second girl is getting into the passenger seat, and the running girl is left on the pavement, waving goodbye with tears in her eyes.

Now when I see Lambton Quay, looking out from the safety of the shop window, there are no long-term visitors other than the weather. In summertime, the brick pathways shine bright, the trees blossom and recoil – then in winter, the wind comes and knocks on the windowpanes, darkness rolls through the night – and still, we keep our doors closed.

I sometimes dream of unlocking the door – that now unfamiliar clewk noise, or was it more of a chicka sound? – ricocheting through the store as I turn the key and let it lift the metal catch. Then, the dream takes on an odd taste, becomes a nightmare – and clewk, I close the dream, the nightmare, the world outside this building, and return to my daily tasks.

It's simple, my job. I spend my days dispensing medications, packaging delivery orders, and organising shelves. No colleagues, one boss – Mr O'Neill. He calls once a week to check in and offer advice based on the database reports and customer reviews sent to him.

'Try to pack the deliveries into the smallest postage parcel you can.'

He likes to verbally make lists.

'Two reasons: a) it saves us money, and b) a lot of the customers are environmentally friendly and would like us to create the smallest amount of waste possible. And remember to start writing personalised notes for orders valued over a hundred dollars.'

And then one Saturday afternoon: 'ChemHouse is offering a half-hour turnaround on deliveries. I think we ought to match it, and once we've mastered that, lower it to twenty minutes. Whaddya reckon, Florence?'

Mr O'Neill is the sort of boss who's a bit useless. All of his ideas come from his competitors. I can tell he wants to be the sort of boss who doesn't need to work anymore, where his money just makes him more money, but he's too bumbling to ever get there. He always says 'whaddya reckon?' as though I'm going to give him a thought-out answer, but I only ever agree. 'Sounds good,' is what I say.

## DELIVERYWOMAN

'To make it happen we might need to trial a new delivery company. Current one's not up to scratch. I'll get back to you with more details,' he replies.

There is no decor in the store. It hasn't been necessary since we stopped needing to impress customers with interior design. It's a regular size, with six shelves that slink their way around the walls, and then three free-standing rows to divide up the floor space. I used to have a coworker, Adriano, but once the number of store visitors dropped to less than five a day, Mr O'Neill let him go. Adriano used to joke that Mr O'Neill was really a clunky robot. 'Seriously, do you know anything about him? Have you ever met him?' he'd say as he scrolled. 'He makes the same mistakes over and over again. Whaddya reckon? Whaddya reckon? Whaddya reckon?'

| | |
|---|---|
| 1 x 20 PK Paracetamol | $12.49 |
| 1 x Prescription Sertraline | $5.00 |
| 2 x ColWall Peppermint Toothpaste | $13.80 |
| 1 x ColWall Electric Toothbrush | $62.00 |
| 1 x Precision Tweezers | $14.50 |
| Total: | $107.79 |
| Notes: | Delivery to doorstep |

I place them into a neat pile, scan each of their barcodes, then pack them into a bubble-wrapped bag in an even neater pile. I slide a piece of branded card across the counter and begin writing a note as instructed.

*Mrs McIntosh,*

*Thank you for your purchase order. As of 16/02/2029, we will be offering a half-hour turnaround on deliveries. I hope you have a lovely day.*

*Kind regards,*

*Florence*

*O'Neills Pharmacy*

⁂

'I've found,' Mr O'Neill begins one afternoon, 'a really top-rated new delivery company.' He sounds like he's reading from a script, and I wonder whether Adriano was right all along, that my only real company is a robot. 'But I don't want to upset the original delivery company. Whaddya reckon?' he continues, but I am too busy watching Contact Island to know whether he actually wants an answer. For a second, I am Mary-Kate, prancing across the beach hand in hand with Ayden, and this life, at this counter, with this telephone between my shoulder and ear, is no longer real. Mr O'Neill is a robot, but then maybe he's an actor, and with an 'are you there?' he becomes my boss again.

'I think there's no harm in trying a new company,' I say.

By the afternoon he has sent around an email, CC'ing all three of the stores he has operating around town with delivery services, notifying us of the trial period.

Normal protocol is to leave delivery packages in the pick-up lot. It's a small passageway with two doors, one from the store and one from the outside. Because we drop them off in the passageway before the deliverers pick them up, we don't even get so much as a breeze of un-air-conditioned-air. But this time, because they're new and don't yet have keys, Mr O'Neill instructs us to let them inside. I feel a jolt inside of me when I read it. I haven't let someone inside the store in months – not since the electrics had to be rewired. Even then, I spent most of their visit hiding in my bedroom in the back, coming out only when they needed assistance.

'I want you to make sure they understand that we're offering a premium service, and so theirs should match it,' Mr O'Neill wrote before signing off.

🌲

When I first meet her, she tells me her name is Mila. She has a crown of brown curls and freckles running off her face. She doesn't scare me, but there is something inside of me that says: this is her. It's an absurd thought. Her as in who?

'So... you live here alone?' she says as she stacks the packages onto her trolley.

'Yeah.'

'Crazy.'

'Guess so. Don't you live alone too?'

'Yeah,' she shrugs, 'but I move around.' The packages look off-balance, and I have an urge to re-stack them. When I raise my hands as though getting ready to catch something if it falls, she raises her eyebrows and wheels her first load away.

🌲

It started slowly, then all at once, when I was nineteen. To begin with, everyone thought it was because the pandemic put life online – work, lectures, funerals, weddings, drinks with friends – and then when the threat of the virus became a distant memory, some said it was because the one percent had pushed the rest into capitalist burnout. Mostly, I think we just became frightened of living. Risk became something to be managed years in advance. Emotional expression was no longer respected, admired, sought after, but instead thought of as embarrassing, overly earnest, or weak.

I still remember the last time I think I witnessed bravery in person, a month or so before I closed the doors. It was on a bus, and two women were sitting in front of me, discussing their love for one another. Woman A was crying, 'I've spent most of my adult life trying not to miss you but missing you anyway,' and going on to apologise for leaving Woman B all those years ago. Woman B reciprocated, and then reminded Woman A of her actual wife, 'You love her, you have a life with her.' Woman A nodded and continued to cry, then began to beg for Woman B to get off at the same stop as her. Woman B was very calm and said no. 'I'll leave her for you,' Woman A said, but Woman B only looked out the window with a glazed expression. Woman A got off in a hurry. It seemed to me that Woman B just no longer loved Woman A. It was only when I stood to get off at my own stop that I turned around and saw Woman B, still looking out the window, with long silent tears streaming down her face.

This was the type of bravery the world had come to admire. Bravery for the self, bravery for the individual.

Technology, everyone's least favourite word and favourite companion, is another of the things people liked to point fingers at. Never-ending reality TV, video games comprising universes, apps for every urge, movement, or thought, virtual reality, interactive films, AI conversations that left you feeling genuinely heard, meant the outside world only posed as a depository of unknown anxieties.

When the amount of sick leave became exorbitant, and the number of visitors became less and less, business owners started to shut their doors – move operations inside. Now even the ones with oceans of cash live as hermits. Restaurants no longer offer dine-in, there is no such thing as shop browsing, and no one can see a movie at the cinema. I have heard of smaller towns of elderly people around the island that still have community centres. But in the cities, workers are given bedrooms in the same building if they're required to work with stock, like me, and the people with jobs that require them to move around are called essentials. There are only three types of essentials: deliverers, film crews, and labourers that either work in hospitals, factories or on infrastructure. When I was young, I wanted to make costumes for films, but now I can't think of anything worse. You need a thick skin to work as an essential.

Now, when I look at Mila, loading up the last of the packages, I can tell her skin isn't physically thick. It looks translucent in some light, blue veins shining through like some kind of highway map leading me somewhere. Thick-skinned in the non-literal sense? Sure. She crashes in and out of the store so unafraid I'm worried she might break something.

🙵

Over the phone, Mr O'Neill tells me that the delivery protocol will be changing permanently, and that Mila will continue to come into the store for delivery pick-ups from now on. 'She thinks it will make the whole process a lot quicker if she can bypass the delivery door. Says it takes her a good few minutes to unlock and relock it, so if she comes in through the front, she can load everything much faster. And pick up any last-minute deliveries you mightn't have had time to drop outside.' This logic makes no sense to me. I feel my mouth open a little, preparing to say something, but then I close it.

While I wait for order notifications to flash on the screen, I busy myself watching season forty-seven of Contact Island. Mary-Kate is telling the camera she doesn't think Ayden is easy-going enough for her. I agree, something about the way he looks when he laughs feels forced, like he's acting. Her breasts are firm and tan, immovable beneath the thin triangles of hot pink stretching across them.

'So, Mary-Kate is getting tired of Ayden,' the strong-accented host bellows over a quick GoPro shot of a tropical beach. 'Let's see what's happening, back at the villa.'

The screen cuts to four women sitting around a fire pit, discussing whether they're moving too quickly with their respective partners.

'I heard they receive intensive training before going on that show,' Mila says.

I jump, but she ignores my fright. 'God knows why they do it, months of being taught to live with other people just so they can become soft porn,' she continues.

'It's hardly soft porn.'

'Why do you watch it then?'

'It's interesting, seeing how they interact with each other.'

'Wouldn't it be a whole lot more interesting if they did it in real life?'

When I look up, she's looking right at me, smiling, waiting for something.

'Do you—?' I begin.

'No.'

'?'

'Yes.'

'?????'

I return to the screen, unsure what it is I'd intended to ask her. Something menial – where she lives, or her age. Then, she tells me she'll pick me up after dropping off the last load of deliveries.

'I can't,' I start, but she is already at the door.

⁂

I spend half an hour in my bedroom looking through the clothes I've had in storage. Eventually I decide upon a black top and a pair of jeans. It's the most dressed up I've been in as long as I can remember, which I believe is saying something.

When she honks, I stay seated on the edge of my bed. I will wait for her to come inside, I decide, so that I can explain in person that I will not be leaving.

When she enters, she yells 'Florence? Ready yet?'

'Coming,' I call, and re-enter the pharmacy.

She is standing by the delivery door, a little pink in the face, like she has rushed to get here.

'Hey,' I say. 'I'm really sorry. But I can't.'

'Why?'

'It's been a while. Years, actually.'

She walks over to me. There is something in the way she moves, like her hips lead the rest of her.

'Why?' she says again.

I can't tell if her eyes are green or blue, but they are large. I look into them, then away, at what I can see of the outside. There is the patchworked brick of the pathway, the beginning of a lamp post, and what used to be a bus stop. I try to think of a reason that is both honest and not as pathetic as I feel. And the truth is, I myself don't know. It feels like the decision has been made by someone else, and I am incapable of making my own. Like I am one organism in a hive of others, and somebody has decided that staying inside is what we do. The alternative feels too solitary, and yet, this hive mentality is the loneliest of them all. 'Being alone, inside, is easier than going out there,' is what I say. 'I like it here. I like my routine.'

She half smiles. 'It's difficult,' she begins, then pauses. 'But life is supposed to be difficult.' Her eyes flicker back to me, then seem to focus on my chin, her lids hanging half-closed.

I feel something warm bloom inside of me, in my cheeks,

between my legs, shivering through to the ends of my fingertips. 'Why though?' is all I can muster.

'Just the way it is. Always has been, always will. Try to think of something beautiful, something miraculous, that doesn't involve some kind of pain.'

I look around the pharmacy, as if an answer might be hiding between the rows of machine-manufactured pills. 'Hmm,' I say.

'Childbirth, for one,' she smiles. 'I read the other day that giving birth is the pain equivalent of breaking twenty bones at once.'

'But, modern medication,' I interject. 'Helps.'

'Agreed, but just because something covers it up doesn't mean it's not still there.' She looks around her as though also looking for inspiration. 'Love,' she mumbles. 'Heartbreak.'

She slots her hand into mine before I even have a chance to notice. Her palms are warm, but the tips of her fingers are cold. I keep my eyes trained on the floor, and when I look up, she is looking me directly in the eyes. I open my mouth to say something, and then we are kissing. It feels both alien and like the most natural thing in the world. Moving, giving, taking, without thought. As easy as riding a bicycle, or even easier, like putting one foot in front of the other. The last time I kissed someone would have been my ex-boyfriend, over seven years ago, and I think about this as our lips continue to interlock. It had been a goodbye kiss, an I-don't-love-you-anymore kiss. This thought drifts away, and others continue to move in and out, like honey, and still we continue to kiss. I feel the strict blocks of thought in my mind melting, dissipating, and the warmth inside growing. Our bodies draw closer. I feel an urge for the place where our hearts are located to match up, as if we are both charging stations for the other. When we pull away, we are both smiling, on the edge of laughter.

'Can we go now?' she says, and I nod.

She opens the door and steps outside first. I feel my heartbeat pause as I try to tell my legs to go. It is the same feeling of standing on the edge of a wharf, and trying to jump, but something invisible keeps constraining you. Your heart lifts up, ready to go, and then sits back down. I feel my mouth doing it too – trying to say something, about to open, about to exclaim it's not possible – but then it is happening, and I'm outside. I'm not sure if I take a single breath on my way to Mila's car. All I know is that I am suddenly at the passenger door, grabbing at the handle.

⁂

We drive through the empty arteries of the city in silence. Most of the buildings I used to know are bare now, but she assures me a lot of the old spots are still in their original places.

'Aunty Mena's?' I ask.

'Yep, but they bought out the building next to it so their whole family could live onsite.'

'Logan Brown?'

'They've scraped through.' She turns the stereo down a notch.

'What about—?'

'They're there, too. Honestly,' she pauses to sigh. 'Everything's still here. Night N Day is probably the only one that went under. Everyone just orders from supermarkets now.'

'Do you order from supermarkets?'

'Have to,' she beams. 'But at least I get to be the one that picks up my order.'

She gives her wheel a squeeze and smiles as it releases a honk, then slides her hand onto my thigh. The strange thing about the streets being deserted is that you can have sex in the car, parked on what used to be the main stretch, before another delivery vehicle rolls by. I come in an embarrassingly short time, her fingers gently jolting inside, sighing with me.

'Sorry,' I gasp.

'Why would you be sorry,' she says, before tucking her lips into mine. Her mouth is warm and wet. 'You should get out more often,' she whispers.

▲

Mila lives in a low-ceilinged apartment at the top of Cuba Street. It's filled with weathered royal furniture – a forest-green velvet couch, a long dining table adorned with candelabras, and the walls are scattered with photographs.

'The best thing about delivering,' she says as she spins the cap of a wine bottle off, 'is that you can afford a bit of luxury.'

It's true. My pay rate covers food, subscription fees, and drycleaning. A portion of my pay is deducted for rent and electricity. If there's a spare dollar it goes towards emergency funds. Still, if I were to be admitted to hospital, I'd have to take out a loan. Delivery jobs, on the other hand, pay well. It's clear in the way Mila can afford an entire apartment to herself, and the wine she's pouring.

'Cheers,' she says.

'Cheers.'

There's no television, no game console – not even a projector. So we sit opposite one another and talk.

'Where did you grow up?' she asks.

'Kilbirnie,' I reply, taking a sip. 'You?'

'Gisborne.'

'Sunny up there.'

'Everyone always says it's sunny,' she laughs.

My cheeks flush a little. 'Sorry,' I say. 'I don't know much about it.' It begins to dawn on me, sitting there in that apartment, that I have not the faintest clue how I've managed to get where I am.

'Hey, sorry. I didn't mean to be rude. My mum always told me I can be confrontational.'

'It's okay.'

'No, really. Sorry,' she pauses to wipe what must be wine from the corner of my lip.

We spend the night with our noses nearly touching and our limbs intertwined. I'm unsure what I want – only that I don't want to spend the night without her.

🔺

The next morning, she says goodbye before the sun has risen. 'There's coffee in the kitchen for you when you need it,' she says, planting gentle kisses all over me while I smile in my sleep. When my own alarm rings, the sun is halfway through its ascent, and the buildings I can see from her window all have orange tints in their reflections. I'm reminded of high school, of how we used to chase sunsets and rises as if it were the only thing in the world left to do.

Outside, the air is sharp, packed tightly with something I have to take a few moments to adjust to. I begin to walk, my shoes slapping softly against the concrete path I used to walk along after school to get to the bus stop. For a moment, I forget which way to go, then it returns to me. Straight down Cuba, left on Manners, right on Willis. Lambton. I have to stop multiple times to take in what's around me. I see no one the whole way home. Once I'm through the doors, the air conditioning feels suffocating. There, on the screen by the counter, is Mary-Kate, sipping an iced coffee. I feel hollow as I watch her watching Hazel, the newest addition to the show.

Mila visits the store three times that day, and each time the shift in the air feels palpable, as if by entering the same room she's charged it with anticipation, like my whole being has been waiting for her.

'Ms Florence,' she jokes, getting down on one knee, 'would you like to accompany me tonight on a series of deliveries?'

I look at her like I am swimming inside of her.

🌲

She picks me up half an hour after my shift finishes. This time I don't wait for her inside, but walk out to the car when I see her pulling up. 'Look at you go,' she laughs. I was so absorbed with looking out the window last time that I didn't notice the stuff in her car – a pile of books in the backseat, whistles hanging from the rearview mirror, and a lucky clover sticker peeling off the glove box. We wind our way through the streets, trees bending over us like fingers, until we reach the bottom of Mount Victoria. The skinny villas the council used to call character homes are now so boarded up they look like wooden rectangles.

'First stop, Quaid's,' she says, jiggling the gear stick into park. 'Want to come with?'

'You need help?'

'Na, just so you can meet him. I'm only dropping off his supermarket order.'

'You go in?'

'Don't look so shocked,' she chuckles. 'He's okay with it.'

As we're standing on his doorstep, I'm sure she can hear my heart racing. The door is covered in fat bubbles, the paint lifting and blistering.

'Hey,' she says. 'You can go back to the car if you'd like.'

I'm about to tell her it's okay when I hear the latch of the lock lifting inside. There, standing in the doorway, is a boy with long brown hair, no older than twenty, wearing a T-shirt with a tiger's face on its front.

'Rawr,' he grins. 'Who've we got here?' His eyes are small, pink and stoned. I like him almost immediately. 'Come on in,' he swings the door open wide, welcoming Mila into a hug. Then he turns to me, 'I've heard about you, pharmacy girl. Bring it in,' and he hugs me too.

'We've only got ten minutes before the next delivery is due, so make it quick,' Mila wags her finger jokingly.

'Ah yes, the grand tour,' he grins, before grabbing my hand and whisking me through the house. 'That's Kahu's room, and this is mine, and that's Fraser's.' The whole house, including the bedrooms, is littered with ashtrays and abandoned mugs. Half-finished board games are strewn on most of the surfaces. It feels lived in, in a way I'd forgotten about.

We continue on this way, Mila carting me around the city to her deliveries, delegating what spare time we have to her favourite people. There's Calypso the batty cellist, Ginny with her triplets, Thomas the ex-philosophy lecturer. By the time we're back on her couch, there are so many sentences spilling out of me we don't kiss till we're in bed.

🌲

'What do you mean, you're quitting?' Mr O'Neill snaps into the phone. 'Things are just starting to pick up.'

'I just don't like it here anymore.'

'Don't like it?'

'I'm not alive when I'm here.'

'Not alive when you're here,' he scoffs. 'You remember Adriano, don't you?' When he says this, I know what he means – remember how Adriano had no job.

'Yes.'

'You want to turn out like that?'

'It's okay, I've got a job,' I breathe.

'A job?'

'I'm joining the delivery team.'

'The delivery team?' he says. 'You know you'll have to go outside a lot for that.' He sounds worried on my behalf when he says this. For the first time, I try to imagine what Mr O'Neill looks like. I see an old man with crow's feet that drag the corners of his eyes down. He looks sad. I try to imagine where he lives but can only see him seated at a desk.

'Mr O'Neill?' I say.

'Yes?'

'Do you have a family?'

'I do. Two daughters, one son.'

'That's nice.'

We fall silent, and the phone lets out a couple of crackles.

'It's lonely, being alone,' I say eventually. 'I think I'll combust if I stay here any longer.'

⁂

I move into Mila's that afternoon. We fill her backseat with boxes and strap the rest to the roof of her car. The last time I moved was when I'd been asked to live in the store. I was living with two friends at the time, Tyla and Molly, but they'd been too anxious to come outside and help me load up the rental truck. It had been a still, calm day. The streets were almost empty, and I'd ridden in the back with my stuff instead of sitting in the passenger seat next to the driver. I kept in touch with Tyla and Molly over video afterwards, the three of us in our respective front camera boxes, until one day we ran out of things to talk about and started sending each other memes about the television shows we were watching instead.

Mila makes room in her drawers for my clothes and presents a new set of coat hangers for me to put my shirts on. Days flit by, then weeks. I'm like a magnet anchored to her. In the night, I wake to find her arms around me. During the day we make our rounds, dropping off clingfilm-wrapped parcels and boxes plastered with address stickers. It takes a while for this rhythm to become natural to me, the stop-start way of the car as we cross each destination off, but then, like realising fluency in a language, I wake up one day and it's there.

🔺

I have never known whether I believe in love. From an early age, I decided there were far simpler things to believe in, like statistics – the optimal amount of sleep to get each night, how to tie your shoelaces – and finances. Two plus two becomes four. Wash your hair twice a week and it will be clean enough. Silk pillowcases retain natural oils for your face. Twenty-one degrees is the prime room temperature for the human body. Up against those involving love – do they love me as much as I love them? How do I know they won't leave me? Do I love the way they make me feel, or do I love them for who they are? What is love? – it is hard to choose love.

Yet, the problem with love, and the reason it seems to persist, is that sometimes it chooses you. When I look at Mila, any time of the day, I feel something inside of me that can't be explained. I search for logical reasons anyway. I read articles on the oxytocin hormones your brain releases when you see someone you love. On the primal instinct to procreate, and the way the human body creates the bonding honeymoon phase to initiate this. It doesn't seem to matter that Mila and I will never have any hope of falling accidentally pregnant – and reducing it to science doesn't help. There are days where things she does annoys me, the way she taps her foot, or whistles in the shower, or doesn't ever make the bed, but they are readily taken over by waves of affection. I have never felt this way, I think, looking back on previous relationships. The way I want to watch her grow old – prune and wrinkle. The way I want to hold her hand when she's sick. The way I want to be there when she tries to quit smoking, or needs somebody to read a book aloud to her when she's had a bad day.

⁂

'So, what's your shtick, pharmacy girl?' Quaid asks during one of our drop-offs. He says it warmly, like he's trying to get to know me better, but something about it catches me off guard.

'Who says shtick?' Mila laughs.

'You know, what's your thing,' he says. 'Everyone has a thing.'

We're sitting at his dining table, waiting for the next delivery request. Mila's flicking through one of his photo albums, and I catch glimpses of people with their arms around one another as she turns the pages.

'I don't really have one,' I mumble. 'I've never been particularly talented, if that's what you mean.'

'Na, I don't mean talent. I mean…' he puts his hands behind his head as though he's reclining on a lounge chair. 'What gets you going?'

'You mean like angry?'

'Yeah, or excited. Something fiery,' he clenches both his fists and brings them to his chest, near where I imagine his heart would be.

'I don't know,' I say. 'I prefer not to think about it.'

Quaid bends over a stained bong and lights a cone. Water begins to bubble and the tube fills with thick, creamy, smoke.

'There's gotta be something you like,' he says, leaving the smoke curling at the opening, before bending over and inhaling again.

Mila looks up from the photo album. 'She likes Contact Island,' she offers.

I find myself studying Quaid's face for a reaction, but there is not a lot he gives away. I can feel the beginning pangs of embarrassment. I look out the window, at the trees moving in the gale winds, at the speed of the clouds moving overhead. I try to think of something to add, but when truth has been told as it just has, there is not much you can say to conceal it. 'Yeah,' I shrug, feigning calm. In truth, I am not embarrassed about not having a respectable passion, but of my own lack of conviction. I know plenty of people who love celebrities, movies, apps, the quick-changing tides of fashion trends, and are defiant about it. I am simply passive, neutral, uncomplicated. And yet, the contradiction in being so uncomplicated is that you become more complicated than those with a clear view of themselves.

When I was small, and my parents would argue a terrible amount, I would hide in the top shelf of the closet in my bedroom. I could still hear them yelling, but it felt like I entered a small pocket of another world. In this world, there was nothing I had to do. I was without body, personality, and responsibilities. Floating, safe, translucent. Undiscoverable, without fear. I would stay tucked in there for hours, with a small torch and sometimes a book. When I grew up and told friends of this habit, they always called it cute. Now, the older I grow, the more I notice patterns. This cupboard became the bedroom at the pharmacy, just as Mila has become each of them combined.

⁂

One morning, I wake earlier than her and tiptoe off to make coffee. When I come back, she's still buried beneath the duvet, the sheet gathered around her left foot.

'Are you sick?' I ask her, but she only groans in reply. 'We've got to head off in twenty, come on,' I smile as I say it, crawling over her on my hands and knees until I'm straddling her above the blanket. She draws it back and taps her cheek lightly, so I lean in to kiss it.

'I can't be fucked,' she grumbles into her pillow. Sunlight beams through the window and crawls across her face.

'Come on,' I say, pulling the blankets back more. 'I can't do it alone.'

'Shhh,' she says, lifting a hand to my face while her eyes are still closed. With gentle fingers, she makes her way around my features – nose, cheek, forehead, chin. Mila opens her eyes. 'Hey,' she smiles.

'Hi,' I tuck a piece of hair behind her ear.

'I can't do today,' she says, bringing the blanket over her mouth. She nudges her nose into a feather that's escaped, avoiding eye contact.

'What do you mean?'

'I just need to hibernate for a bit. Nothing serious. I'll be fine tomorrow.' She lifts the blanket over her head.

'Okay,' I say.

'I love you,' she muffles through the bedding.

'I love you.'

It takes a while for me to convince myself, standing there in the kitchen, to do the deliveries alone. I go back to the bedroom three times before finally accepting she's not changing her mind. All of a sudden, I want to be far, far away, in anyone's world but mine. It dawns on me that this life is no different from the last, that all I've done is replace the channel I'm tuned into. When she's not switched on, I'm back to square one.

In the car, I want to cry. This is a different breed of loneliness, I think, walking my eyes along the dashboard of the car, pausing on items that belong to her. An abandoned keychain, and those same whistles knotted around the neck of the rear-view mirror. This is a different breed of loneliness because it is the moment after saying goodbye to someone you love. Like when you are waving goodbye to your Mum, Dad, friends, and you can see still see them, and so you continue to wave, until they're gone, and you continue standing there, wondering if they will turn back, and maybe they do, but there is still a corner they must turn and a resting position your hand must find, and a walk of your own you must do, back to the car or inside the house. I click the delivery tracker on and watch as the screen fills with notification bubbles. The day's schedule seems quiet, as I scan the list, mainly grocery shops, until I see a familiar location appear – O'Neill's Pharmacy. I feel my cheeks grow a little pink, and then put it aside, and begin my route to the supermarket on the waterfront. As I pull into the empty car park, I am reminded of my visits as a child, when I would go there with school friends to get snacks for the cinema. Strange, I think, lifting shopping bags into the car, how memories can layer on top of one another. How easy it is to focus only on the surface. Strange, I think as well, eventually snaking my way back through the streets to the pharmacy, how easily I had turned my back on my home of six years. It wasn't that there was much to be sentimental about, but that I had somehow both mentally blanked and managed to avoid driving near it, or even past it, that fascinated me. Parked outside, I looked at the glass box with equal sorrow and intrigue. I tried to imagine what Mila must have seen that first day she visited, what on Earth had compelled her to want to be close to me. I would have come across so charmless, so unexciting.

I walk to the front door and see a newly installed delivery chute. I imagine Mr O'Neill on the phone with my replacement – 'No contact but the speed of contact! Whaddya reckon? Whaddya reckon?' – and giggle to myself. Then I see the legs of somebody on the other side of the chute, pushing parcels through. I look up, and—

'Florence?' he laughs. 'No fucking way.'

'What the hell!' I laugh back. He looks older, thinner, but still very much himself. 'Adriano?'

Our voices muffle through the glass, and we both smile and wave our hands about like birds.

He mimes unlocking the door. 'Do you want to come in?'

'Sure,' I nod.

The inside of the pharmacy hasn't changed, save for the absence of my things and the addition of his. He makes us cups of tea. There is still only one seat for the till desk, and so we sit on the floor. Him with his legs crossed, mine tucked into my chest.

'How have you been? Mr O'Neill said you were delivering now, but I couldn't really believe it.'

'I've been good – okay. I've been okay.'

'And?'

'Well, I met someone,' I smile.

The conversation continues quietly. He tells me about his life, how he moved back home to his dad's after he was let go, how he became depressed and found it difficult to leave his bed for about two years. 'You know I have always despised work. But there is no denying it – it gives you something to get up for.' He turns away. 'It's difficult looking back on that time,' he says. 'I'm not proud of how bad it got.' It's the most serious I have seen Adriano's face – I have always remembered him with the expression of someone who's trying to hold in laughter.

'I couldn't even tell you what I did with my days. I was unemployed for five years. I know the television was on most of the time, but it was like I was plugged into it, waiting to be charged, only I could never get past thirty percent. I was too tired to be sad. Too sad to be tired. God, look at me,' he laughs, and tears begin to dribble down his cheeks. 'The funny thing is,' he laughs again. 'I'm actually really good now. Well, you know, good enough. I've figured out how to hang out with myself properly. And I go outside! Every day.'

'God, that's good,' I reply. 'Where do you go?'

'Up into the Green Belt. All the way up to Mount Victoria. Sometimes out to Princess Bay. Or into the Tararuas.'

'I was imagining Oriental Bay.'

'You've got to get out of the city, that's the trick,' he sniffs. 'What's crazy is the people you run into. Still only a few, but more than you'd realise.' He laughs again. 'My theory is everyone got so anxious they had to go inside, and then so much more anxious they had to go outside.'

When I return home, Mila's out of bed and sitting at the dining table, staring sadly into space. 'Hey,' I say.

'Hey.'

'Guess who I saw today,' I shuffle onto the bench opposite where she is sitting. She looks tired, two lines drawing the skin under her eyes into bags.

'Who?'

'Adriano, my old workmate.'

'Oh. How is he?'

'Good, I mean, he's had a rough time. But he's so much better.'

'That's good,' and then, 'Flo?'

It is not in the way she says it, or her expression, but as if somehow the admission brewed long before I arrived and is already hanging in the air between us.

'Yeah?'

'I think I want to go,' she says slowly. 'I think I want to leave.'

'Where?' but I already know. Anywhere but here.

'Anywhere but here.'

'Why? Are you unhappy?'

'No. Yes, maybe. But with you,' she spreads her arm across the table between us, leaving her hand palm up, waiting to be held. 'I want to go with you.' She looks at me sadly, then out the window. 'When I was little,' she begins. 'I never used to be able to sleep. My mum was strictly into herbal remedies. The homeopath did all these natural tests. They found this flower called the Happy Wanderer. Told me I liked to move, that I liked change, that too much of one thing would ruin me.'

I feel my organs sinking. I consider arguing. I think about denouncing herbal remedies, but before I've even considered what to say, I feel resignation settling within me. This was always going to happen, I think. I have known this all along. Something good might happen to me but then it will leave.

'You know I can't come with you,' I say.

'But that's not true,' she pleads.

I can already feel the workers inside my mind busy at work, building a wall between my answer and the others. 'It is,' I reply.

We spend hours combing through why we each feel the way we feel, and with each small admission of truth, it becomes impossible not to feel hurt. The more she speaks about the world outside of our own the more I feel I am being left behind. The more I speak about my need to stay the more she feels she is being ignored. That night, we make love, but in a desperate sort of way, in a way I wish we hadn't.

In the morning, smoking a cigarette on the balcony while Mila is still sleeping, I think about the women on the bus that day, of whether it was Woman A leaving Woman B by getting off the bus, or Woman B leaving Woman A by remaining seated. I used to think it was undoubtedly the former. I used to think choosing to remain somewhere, to say no, to protect oneself, was the only admirable thing one could do. I wonder whether this is because it was a departure from the original. Chasing someone to the airport was romantic until it became a cliché, just as asking someone to love you back became begging. I'm still not sure whether I want to do these things. But not doing them – remaining seated, and looking out the window, crying – I'm now no longer sure whether that is bravery, or just cowardice. The line between chasing love and protecting yourself can be very fine. It is true, the way I was taught in History lessons, that the world moves in circles. Too much in one direction dips you into the other. Loving someone too much becomes selfish, just as not loving someone enough also does. The method of getting it right is what terrifies me into paralysis. It is much easier to watch and judge than it is to take your own leap of faith.

She is still asleep when I go back inside. I kiss her softly on the forehead, then grab my things and head out. I get into the car and stick the key into the ignition. While I wait for the engine to warm, I click the delivery tracker on. There are twelve deliveries loaded so far, the first pick-up just a few blocks away. I turn left, right, then left again, until the car's chugging at a standstill just outside the electronics store I'm scheduled to collect a phone charger from. But I can't do it. I feel in my gut that it's wrong. Like there is a God after all, and they're telling me to keep going. I lift my foot off the brake, then press hard on the accelerator, the engine jolting back to life as I drive down the street, towards the water. Every time I'm at a crossroads I ask my mind left or right? Left, it says. Then, right. I follow it. The tracker is buzzing with a late notice. If I drove off the wharf, what would it mean? No, that's not it. How about a field, spin myself through the mud? That's not it either. Soon enough, I'm on the motorway, catapulting myself along the coast at 120 kilometres an hour. I feel like a bullet. There will be no left or right turns until I reach the top of the island. I could drive through the night, if I wanted to. Hours fade away. The sun sets for a long time, until it is just me and the lights of the driver's panel. Outside, the darkness becomes darker and deeper, until I am no longer sure what direction is bush and what direction is urban, save for the small squares of light that appear every so often, lit up yellow and orange, to let me know there are in fact bedrooms within homes within roads, connected to the very one I'm on. It comforts me in that same way Christmas lights do, or streetlamps. It comforts me because they guide me somewhere outside of myself, that in turn, takes me back inside. Up the veins of Mila's arms, or along a walkway.

## ACKNOWLEDGEMENTS

It is a surreal and wonderful thing to sit down and think about everybody who has played a part in the formation of this book.

Firstly, an enormous thank you to Tina Makereti and the International Institute of Modern Letters for such a marvellous year in 2021. It's one I will never, ever, forget. Thank you to my supervisor, Anna Taylor, for the frequent hugs, kind advice, and always encouraging us to sit on the floor.

Thanks to our class – Aline Tran, Nkhaya Paulsen-Moore, Tamara Tuliatua, Charlotte Doyle, Jono McLeod, Caroline Ziemke-Dickens, Melody Chang, and Callum Knight. It was the utmost privilege to read your work, and to still be such close friends.

Thank you to my brilliant agent, Kirsty McLachlan, for your unflinching support and for finding the right home for this collection. Thank you to Gary Budden from Influx Press for taking it on with such enthusiasm, and for your insightful edits.

Thank you to the short story writers who have been guiding lights for this collection – Airini Beautrais, Jonas Eika, George Saunders, Carmen Maria Machado, Hilary Leichter, Ling Ma, and Laura Van Den Berg.

Thank you to the editors of the publications and websites where some of these stories have previously appeared in various forms: *Food Court Books*, *Journal of Dreams*, *Mayhem Literary Journal*, and the *National Library of New Zealand*.

Thank you to the places and people that have housed me while writing these stories – to Alyson, Chris and Margaret for the time I was able to spend at the Martinborough writers' cottage, to Caitlin and Nick for lending me your little red home in Waikawa, to the IIML for the writing rooms (and their view of the ocean), and to so many lovely libraries – particularly the Grey Lynn library and Peckham library.

Thank you to the friends who have also been close and trusted readers – Lucy Brewerton, Miles Fox, Olly Campbell, and Emma Houpt. A special thank you to Sam Knegt, who was the first voice of encouragement when I was starting to take writing more seriously.

Thanks to Fariha Róisín, and the Catapult class of 2019 – Hayley Mojica, Jenny Lee, Madhuri Sastry, Alisha Wexler, Monica Jamaluddin, Kristen Poli, Nia Wilson, and Jungwon Lee – for helping me gain the confidence I needed to keep writing.

Thank you to my Mum and Dad, for always believing in me and encouraging me to be curious – and to my beloved friends and family, who have supported me with life. It's because of all of you that this has been possible.

## ABOUT THE AUTHOR

Eva is a graduate of Te Herenga Waka – Victoria University of Wellington and the MA programme in fiction at the International Institute of Modern Letters, where she worked on a short-story collection that received the Jean Squire Project Scholarship. She was also taught by Fariha Róisín in a Catapult writing programme in New York. Her writing has been featured in *The Dominion Post, Food Court Books, Mayhem Literary Journal, Turbine | Kapohau, The National Library of New Zealand, Journal of Dreams, Silo Theatre,* and others. She is originally from Aotearoa New Zealand and is currently based in London.

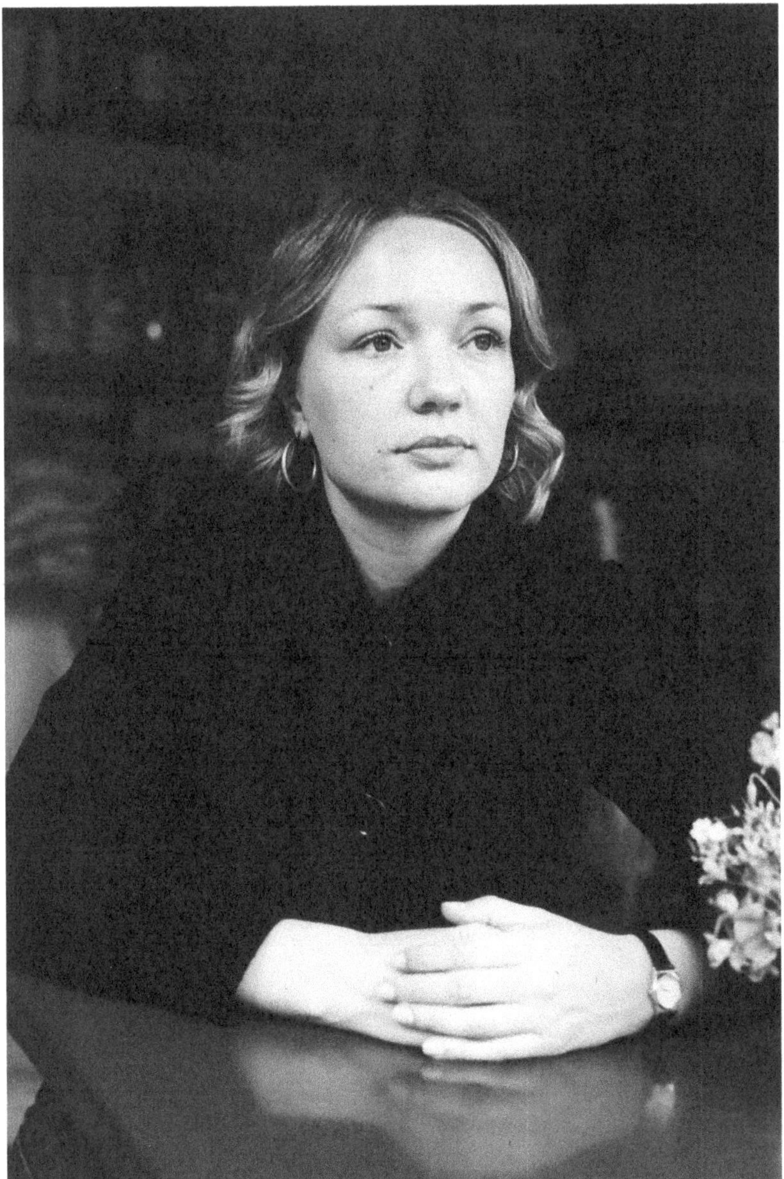

**INFLUX PRESS**

Influx Press is an award-winning independent publisher based in London, committed to publishing innovative and challenging literature from across the UK and beyond.

www.influxpress.com
@Influxpress

## THANKS TO OUR KICKSTARTER SUPPORTERS

Eva Aldea
Josh Allen
Eleanor Anstruther
Victoria Barkas
Jennifer Bernstein
Freddie Bonfanti
Matthew Colbeck
Amanda Dackombe
Marianna Datsenko
Max Edwards
Janet Ference
Jonathan Gibbs
Bill Godber
Gary Grace
Ellie Hawkes
John McCrea
Joanne McNeil
Matt Petzny
Neil D.A. Stewart
Goutham Veeramachaneni
Olivia Wakefield
Andrew Wynn
Teresa Young

## THANKS TO OUR LIFETIME SUPPORTERS

D. Franklin
Barbara Richards
Bob West